Stained Glass

Stained Glass

MICHAEL BEDARD

Tundra Books

Published in Canada by Tundra Books,
481 University Avenue, Toronto, Ontario M5G 2E9

Published in the United States by
Tundra Books of Northern New York,
P.O. Box 1030, Plattsburgh, New York 12901

Library of Congress Card Number: 2001086827

National Library of Canada Cataloguing in Publication Data

Bedard, Michael, 1949-
Stained glass

ISBN 0-88776-552-1

I. Title.

PS8553.E298S72 2001 jC813'.54 C2001-930264-9
PZ7.B381798St 2001

We acknowledge the support of the Canada Council for the Arts and the Ontario Arts Council for our publishing program.

We acknowledge the financial support of the Government of Canada through the Book Publishing Industry Development Program for our publishing activities.

Design by Sari Naworynski

Printed and bound in Canada

1 2 3 4 5 6 06 05 04 03 02 01

M

MMMMMMM

Marvellous Martha

Acknowledgments

A book is a window made of many pieces. For the important pieces they provided, the author thanks Peter Coffman, Paul Costable, Marilyn Joiner, Alex McPhee, Marisha Robinsky, Gerry Tooke, and Kathy Lowinger and the staff at Tundra.

Remembrance has a rear and front –
'Tis something like a house –
It has a garret also
For refuse and the mouse.

Besides the deepest cellar
That ever mason laid –
Look to it by its fathoms
Ourselves be not pursued.

Emily Dickinson

PROLOGUE

The scar began at the base of the nail of his baby finger and ran halfway round. When you stroked it with the thumb of your other hand, there was a strange numbness to it, and when you squeezed the skin, the flesh around it turned red and the line of the scar stood white against it, and you could count how many stitches there were.

When he was sitting thinking, he had a habit of rubbing the scar. He sat rubbing it now, and a memory rose whole and spontaneous in his mind like a genie streaming from a lamp – the memory of a Saturday morning when he was six.

He had awoken early that morning, as usual, and tiptoed quietly down the basement stairs to visit his sister Emily. Everyone else was still asleep, but Emily too was an early riser, and when he woke Saturdays he would often slip downstairs to see her.

Her bedroom was in the basement of the house – a small, low-ceilinged room lined in a wood paneling that made it look like a log cabin. It was somehow fitting that Emily should have this room. For though she lived with them, there was always a part of her that was remote, a secret center of her that dwelt alone in a log cabin in a deep wood, a cabin that only seemed on the outside to be tucked into a corner of the basement in the bungalow they lived in then.

There was a small room next to hers that they called the cold room. Cans and jars lined the wooden shelves, along with all the broken things that Father could not stand to part with. For one day, if only he were given the time, Father would mend all the broken things they had.

One of these broken things was an old mantel clock he had picked up somewhere. With its elegantly styled wooden case, it looked decidedly out of place. But its brokenness made it right at home.

For some reason or other, Emily and he took it into their heads that Saturday morning to try and fix the clock. Normally their Saturday mornings together were not quite so adventurous. They would lie together across her bed and look at books, while the radio played quietly in the background. Sometimes she might read to him. Emily was a wonderful reader – she could draw you into a story and spirit you away. But then, Emily and books had always been friends. Emily and clocks were quite another story.

Now, neither of them had a clue what was wrong with the clock other than that it didn't work, nor did they have the least notion of how to repair it. They didn't let that deter them. They took the clock down from the shelf, cleaned and polished its rich dark wood until it shone and the glass face gleamed, then took it into Emily's room and set it on the bed.

There was a key in the back of the clock. The first thing they did was to wind it. They had, of course, tried that several times in the past without success, so that now, with scarcely two turns, the clock was completely wound and still not working. They next slapped it hard several times to no effect.

They shook it. As always, it responded well to shaking. It ticked contentedly along for almost a minute, then stopped dead. They did this several times, advancing the time by a full five minutes, hoping that the clock would catch on to the pleasure of ticking again. The next time they shook it, it actually kept a good steady tick going for more than two minutes, then suddenly remembered itself and stopped. After that, no amount of shaking would induce it to tick again.

"Stupid bloody thing," said Emily, who could curse with the best of them when she'd a mind to.

She flipped the clock facedown on the bed and examined the back of the case. Four small setscrews held the backing in place. She went to Father's workbench, just outside her room, and came back with half a dozen screwdrivers. The fourth one fit, and in a matter of minutes they had the back of the clock off and lying with the screws on the bed.

The works of the clock were now exposed – a bewildering array of gears and wheels and springs. Emily studied them minutely, touching them tentatively with the screwdriver here and there, as one might prod some felled beast for signs of life.

Theirs was but pretended knowledge. Neither of them had followed in Father's footsteps. He could look at something like this and, by some sure instinct, see the problem instantly. They only looked.

"I think that's the mainspring," said Emily, touching the tip of the screwdriver to a tight coil of metal in the midst of the works. "If we could only figure out how to release the tension a little, we might be able to get it to work."

She prodded it from several angles without success, then worked the end of the screwdriver in around the toothed meshing of metal gears. There was a slight quick motion, and the screwdriver stuck tight in the works.

It could not be budged. The clock lay on the bed like a patient on an operating table with a scalpel stuck tight in his inmost parts. They looked dumbly on – surgeons baffled by the unexpected phenomenon.

"We have a problem here," said Emily.

There were ominous sounds of movement overhead. The rest of the family was beginning to stir. It would not do at all for Father to come down and discover the clock in this state. Their sole intent now was to dislodge the screwdriver, replace the backing, and return the clock to its quiet shelf in the cold room.

"Maybe if you hold the clock down and I yank," she suggested.

There was little place to get a grip on the clock with its backing off without coming into contact with the coiled works. He gripped it as well as he could, but his fingertips felt the cold touch of metal beneath them.

"Ready?" asked Emily, and simultaneously gave a mighty pull on the screwdriver.

Instantly several things happened in quick succession. The sense of succession was a matter of memory, however; at the time, they all seemed to happen at once.

The screwdriver came free and Emily fell back onto the bed with the force of the sudden release. There was a furious whirring of the metal works of the clock, a sound he still recalled with a shudder; then a searing pain as the top of his baby finger was ripped by the whirling teeth of the gears.

He was far too shocked to scream. He pulled his finger free. The nail was torn at the quick and the skin beside it sliced to the bone. There was a brief interlude of bloodlessness, as if the body held its breath – and then the blood flowed.

And how it flowed. Emily's momentary elation at having freed the screwdriver was instantly quenched. She took one look at the finger and sprang up from the bed. She tried to calm him, though she herself was clearly frightened. And still at the forefront of both their minds was the desire to escape detection.

The terror of the instant was encased in silence like a thing in glass. It was this moment of silence he remembered most clearly, as though this was what centered the memory in his mind.

Emily reached for the nearest thing at hand – a satin pillow sham she had bought the year before as a souvenir of a family trip to Niagara Falls. A scene of the Falls embroidered on the satin, a yellow fringe all around. She wrapped it quickly around his finger and closed her hand over it.

"There. It'll be all right, Charles. Don't cry, please. It'll be all right."

He wondered if she really felt it would be. Probably not. She wouldn't have used her pillow sham if she had. Her voice wouldn't have been shaking the way it was.

His finger was throbbing now. Great pulsing waves of pain against the satin sham, her clenched hand.

"It hurts, Emmy. It hurts."

"Damn," she muttered beneath her breath. "Damn. Damn."

With her free hand she slipped the backing of the clock in place, as though hiding the site of the disaster might make things better, coax time back to the before.

After a few minutes, she released her hand from the wound. The pillow sham was soaked through with blood. She unwrapped it. The sight of the blood, of the raw red wound utterly undid him. His stomach pitched, and an icy chill raced through him. He felt like he might fall face-first onto the floor then and there.

Emily must have seen the shape he was in. Later, when they talked about that day, as they often did, she said he'd gone as white as a ghost.

She quickly rewrapped the finger, laid him down on the bed, and sat there beside him stroking his head. Then she did something he'd never seen her do before. She began to cry. Quietly, ever so quietly.

"I'm sorry, Charles," she sobbed. "I'm so sorry."

She got up and ran from the room, and he lay there feeling the cold press of the clock against his ribs, listening to her hurried footsteps on the wooden stairs, and watching the walls of the room pulse to the pain in his finger. His eyes darted around the room, trying vainly to catch at something solid outside himself. Vague thoughts of mortality came into his panicked mind.

It seemed an eternity before Emily returned, with Father in tow. Father was still in his pajamas, his hair flattened on one side from sleep. He had to stoop to get through the doorway. Once he was in, he seemed to fill the room.

He looked at Charles, looked at the clock, and you could see him piece the whole story together in his mind. He didn't get angry; he just knelt down beside the bed and asked Charles to show him his hand. He took one look at it and said he'd need stitches. He asked Emily to give Charles a hand getting dressed, then he hurried off to get dressed himself.

Emily ran to get Charles some clothes from his room. She pulled his pants on carefully over his pajamas, carefully removed his pajama top, and eased on a shirt. He lay there on the bed, feeling dizzy and faint, while she did the buttons up.

By that time, the rest of the household had been alerted. His little brother, Albert, and his twin sister, Elizabeth, appeared by the bed, unusually subdued by the sight of a felled sibling. Albert kept asking him if he'd really chopped his finger off, and he wanted to see the evidence.

Mother's hair was still in pin curls when she appeared by the side of the bed. She was very concerned in her own peculiar way. Mother's response to any mishap was to grow utterly methodical and emotionless. It was she who now took the clock off the bed and carefully gathered up the loose screws. She was troubled that Emily had used the pillow sham, first because it was not very clean, and secondly because the blood probably wouldn't wash out.

She went and got a roll of gauze and a bottle of disinfectant, cleaned the cut, wound and tied the gauze, then put the pillow sham in a pail of cold water to soak. She combed his hair and got his coat on while Father went and got the car. As they were about to leave, she kissed him in a formal way, like a distant relation, and told him everything would be okay.

Emily sat in the backseat with him on the way to the hospital. He lay back on the seat with his head against her shoulder, hoping desperately he would not be sick in the car, on top of everything else.

It took five stitches to close the wound – five rather untidy stitches, for the cut had not been a clean one. A week later the doctor took them out.

1

St. Bart's

At the still point of the turning world.
Neither flesh nor fleshless;
Neither from nor towards; at the still point,
there the dance is. . . .

T. S. Eliot, *Four Quartets*

I

You begin with sand and ash. One part sand, washed in water and cleaned of earth and stones, and two parts ash of beech or fern. Mix these together well, place them in clay pots, and set the pots in the upper portion of the oven. Stir them with a ladle as they heat to keep them from melting. Do this for a night and a day.

Meantime, fashion pots of clay, wide at the top and narrow at the base, with the lip curved in about the rim. Fire these, and in the evening fill them with the frit from the first pots. Set them low in a red-hot furnace and stoke the fire with dry wood all the night long.

By morning, the sand and ash will be fused into molten glass. Let it cool a little, then take the iron blowpipe, put the end in the glass, and when the glass begins to stick, slowly turn the pipe and gather what you need. Take the gather from the fire, bring the open end of the pipe to your mouth, and blow gently, careful to take the pipe from your mouth each time you draw breath, lest by chance you suck flame.

Blow quickly and repeatedly, striking the glowing glass gently against a smooth flat stone until it forms a bladder shape equal on all sides round. Then cut the ends and split the side with a hot iron and return it to a red-hot furnace. When it starts to soften, open it with tongs where it is split, spread it out and flatten it with a smooth stick. When it is completely flat, remove the sheet of glass with tongs to the annealing oven and let it cool slowly so as not to crack. When cooled, it is ready for the making of windows.

From the twelfth century treatise by Theophilus, "The Art of the Worker in Glass," in his *De Diversis Artibus*

2

The clock mounted on the face of the organ loft made a muted click as it measured off another minute. Charles glanced up at it – 4:30. It would soon be safe to leave for home.

The inside of the old church was dim. The only light came through the stained glass windows that ran along both sides of the nave. For the first few minutes after you walked in, it felt as if you'd come into a cave walled in colored glass. But as your eyes adjusted to the lower light, the space took shape around you. The ribbed vaulting of the ceiling stole from the shadows. Creatures carved in stone peered down from the pillar tops. Patches of flaking paint appeared on the walls.

St. Bartholomew's was an old church that had definitely seen better days. It sat in the midst of what had once been a wealthy neighborhood of tree-lined streets and sedate old houses. Most of the trees had now succumbed to age or disease. The lawns had been bricked over, the houses broken into rooming houses. The old Caledon Psychiatric Hospital stood nearby, and outpatients tended to gravitate to the neighborhood. A lot of lost-looking souls walked the streets: people in their private worlds, broken worlds.

Many of the stores along the main street where the church stood had died, or were looking poorly. Some had been boarded up, others turned into makeshift residences with sheets draped over the inside of the plate glass and withered plants languishing on the windowsills.

He had discovered the church one Friday a couple of months back, shortly after he'd started skipping his piano lesson. It had been a March day, and bitterly cold. After wandering the streets aimlessly, he'd stumbled on the place quite by chance. The door was open, and he'd slipped in and spent half an hour sharing the empty church with a handful of homeless people, also escaping the cold. The silence of the place had shocked him. It was as if he'd breached some boundary between worlds.

At the back of the church, as if by way of welcome, there stood a life-sized statue of St. Bartholomew. St. Bart had been one of the original twelve apostles. Tradition had it that he'd been martyred by being flayed alive. The statue depicted him holding the long hooked knife of his martyrdom in one hand, with the slack pelt of his skin draped over the other arm, the way Gran draped her sweater over her arm when she went out for a walk on a summer evening, in case she got cold.

Often there would be one or two other stray souls scattered through the rows of wooden pews, but today the place seemed empty. Even the caretaker, who could normally be seen flitting quietly along the shadowed aisles as he went about his work, had fled into the sun. Charles had seen him perched on a high ladder outside, washing the windows. He could see the shadow of his arm now, moving silently against the glass, like the beating of some great wing.

His book bag lay on the seat beside him. He opened it and pulled out his piano exercise book, turning to the little Bach piece he was supposed to have been practising. It was simply a question of time before they discovered he'd been skipping the lesson. There were bound to be consequences, but somehow it didn't seem to matter.

Gran had always had a passion for the piano. The ornate old upright had sat in the corner of the dining room for as long as he could remember. One of his first memories was of sitting beside her on the bench while she played. He would bang away on the keys and pretend that he too was playing. She had promised him then that when he was old enough, she would pay for him to take lessons, as his father had taken lessons as a boy.

And so, two years ago, when the bunch of them had moved in with her, she had talked him into going to lessons. But everything had changed by then. He was no longer the little boy banging away on the keys. And though he went dutifully to the lessons and dutifully practised for a long while without complaint, each note cut like a knife, and finally he could do it no more. He knew it would disappoint her, but for his own sake he had to stop.

And so he had simply quit, without bothering to tell anyone he had done it. And now he found himself entangled in a lie, without the courage to extract himself from it, without the words to explain why it had wrenched him apart to play. It was the first really devious thing he'd done in his life, and he still had not recovered from the shock of it. Even now, as the door at the back of the church opened, his heart gave a little flutter and he half expected one of his family to walk in and find him here.

Instead it was a small stooped woman, with a shawl pulled up over her hair. She slipped down the side aisle to the front of the church. A large marble Pietà stood by a side altar there, with a bank of votive candles before it. She rooted through her bag for change, then dropped two coins through the slot of the metal box, touched the taper to a flame, and lit two candles. The taper smoked as she extinguished it, and a thin stream of smoke ascended in the still air. She knelt in the front pew and prayed.

He wondered what she was praying about. He often wondered that about those he saw in the church when he came, for most of them truly were praying, not simply hiding out as he was. Still, he knew that even he was doing more here now than merely hiding out. For some reason he did not fully understand, he was drawn to this old church with its rattling rads and water-stained walls; with its sad-eyed statues and shattered rainbows of light that flecked the floor.

Part of it was the pure strangeness of the place. At the back of the church, tucked in a corner on the wall by the magazine rack, there was an old framed article from the *Caledon Daily Examiner* on the history of St. Bart's. He had read there that the church's first patron, who had donated the parcel of land on which it was built, had willed that on his death his heart be removed and interred in the walls of the church. And so it was done. The heart lay sealed now in a niche in the west wall. Charles had found the stone inscribed in Latin that marked the spot, and had stood there wondering at the strangeness of the heart walled in the stone.

Sometimes he would wander the shadowy aisles, sometimes simply sit in a pew, quietly looking around, while the forty-five minutes of the lesson ticked slowly by. And it was as if he were taking a lesson in silence. He could feel the silence of the place seep into him, in the way the faint smell of incense seeped into his clothes. It seeped into him and woke other silences there.

Once, years ago, after a huge snowstorm had struck Caledon, he and Elizabeth had gone with Emily to toboggan down the steep white hills in the park near their home. It was early on a Sunday morning, and there was no one else around. Theirs had been the first footsteps to break the pure expanse of snow. They were like explorers in a new world. And as they walked side by side through the park, pulling the toboggan along behind them, a hush came over them, and he felt the silence enfold them, tucking them under its great white wing.

There was something of that long-ago snowfall here still in this empty church, as though all the silences in the world were heaped in drifts around him here.

3

George Berkeley did not like heights. His legs felt queer, all cobbled together with wood and wire like a marionette's, as he clung to the upper rungs of the ladder. He dunked the dirty rag into the pail of soapy water suspended from the ladder and wrung it out, careful not to look down.

He was working his way along the east wall of the church, washing the outside of the stained glass windows. There were six windows in all, dingy with the dust and soot that had settled on them over the years. He had finished the first three and was starting on the fourth. He would do just this one more, he told himself, as he had told himself with each of the others, and that would be it for the day.

He gripped the rung of the ladder with one hand and leaned as far as he dared to reach the far side of the window with the rag. The soapy water ran down the glass and pooled on the sill.

From the outside the window looked lifeless. Dull bits of glass webbed with lead. A stranger passing on the street would not even have known what scene the window depicted. Yet, from within, where the sun's light shone through, the window woke and was all alive.

This was the St. Francis window, likely the oldest window in Caledon. He suspected that this and the one that faced it across the nave were medieval in origin, though the experts were skeptical that such rare windows could ever have found their way to Caledon. The consensus of opinion was, rather, that they were fine imitations of ancient glass. No less, but certainly no more.

Mr. Berkeley knew better. As a young lad in England in the sixties, he and a group of his friends who were going to art school had apprenticed to the glass craftsmen at Canterbury Cathedral. There was a wealth of ancient glass that had managed to survive the centuries at Canterbury, much of it tucked out of harm's way in the upper reaches of the cathedral.

Before the outbreak of the Second World War, the dean of the cathedral, sensing what was in the wind, had all the ancient windows removed and buried in the crypt under six feet of sand to keep them safe.

When the war was over, as one by one the windows were uncovered and returned to their places, they were first restored: stripped of the old leads, the glass washed, then the whole releaded. It was to aid in this work that George Berkeley and his fellow apprentices had been engaged. And in the course of it, he had come to know the ancient glass intimately – the look of it, the feel of it, the play of light upon it. There was no doubt in his mind now as he studied closely the lacework of the old leads, the pitting in the outer surface of the glass, that this window was kin to those he had worked on then.

It was at Canterbury, too, that he had acquired his dislike of heights, perched on the narrow parapet, sixty feet off the ground, the heels of his shoes hanging out over the edge while he anchored the ladder for the master to heft a mended panel back into place.

He ran his rag over the intricate mosaic of glass. The window depicted several scenes from the legend of St. Francis and the Wolf of Gubbio. Here, before its cave, was the great wolf that terrorized the townspeople of Gubbio. Here, strewn on the ground about it, were human bones. There, in the distance, were the walls of the town. He ran the cloth lightly over them. Water dripped lazily from the edge of the rag down to the garden far below, where the feet of the ladder stood anchored in the soft soil.

There upon the path that led from the town through the woods below was Francis, come to meet the wolf. Finally, there was the wolf transformed, placing its paw in the saint's hand as a pledge that it would do harm no more.

So absorbed was Mr. Berkeley in the tale told by the glass that he failed at first to notice that the ladder had begun to edge sideways along the stone. For as he leaned, the soft soil yielded and one of the ladder's feet began to sink into the soil beneath.

By the time he noticed, it was too late. He tried frantically to right the ladder by shifting his weight the other way, thought for one blissful moment that he had managed it, then realized with sick certainty that he was about to fall.

4

What strange magic made him able to hear the Bach piece played whole in his mind as he sat there on the bench looking at the piano exercise book, Charles wondered – so that his eye seemed to strike the notes and the sound rose from the page like the smoke rising in the still air.

The woman had left now, left so quietly he had not heard her go. Once again he was alone.

Suddenly there was a muffled cry, then a loud crash. The lower panel of one of the stained glass windows on the opposite side of the church shattered in a shower of glass. There was a sudden square of sunlight, where before there had been glass. The top of a wooden ladder poked through the hole.

He sat for a moment, stunned. Then, over the startled pounding of his heart, he heard a low moan. It came from the direction of the damaged window. He closed his book, got up, and made his way cautiously over there.

Lying facedown on the bench beneath the broken window was a boy. He lay, unmoving, as though he were dead. Then he made a low moan and slowly turned his head. Instantly Charles realized it was not a boy at all, but a girl not much older than himself. Blood channeled down her cheek from a cut above her eye.

Her clothes were pretty beat up. Her clipped hair was a mass of tangles. She looked like one of those street people who often shared the church with him, sitting in the pews like spirits, their belongings bundled in plastic bags beside them. But this girl was so young. He stood there, wondering what to do. The girl was covered in bits of glass from the broken window. An old guitar, with a length of string for a strap, lay beside her on the bench.

Finally, he leaned down and touched her lightly on the shoulder. Instantly she opened her eyes and looked up at him.

"Who are you?" she asked.

"My name's Charles," he said. "Are you all right?"

She sat up. Bits of glass rained down onto the bench, fell with a light *thrum* onto the strings of the guitar.

"What happened?" she asked.

"The window broke," he said. "I guess you were lying here sleeping, and it fell on you."

She reached up to her forehead and touched the cut above her eye. She looked at the blood on her finger, more with surprise than concern. She began to look about, her eyes lighting first on the windows, then following the line of an arch up to the vault of the ceiling.

"Where are we?"

"We're in St. Bart's. You know, St. Bartholomew's Church. I guess you came in to catch some sleep. Then the window broke and –"

The girl rose, slung the guitar over her shoulder, and squeezed past him into the aisle. She walked slowly to the front of the church, looking around her all the while, running her hand repeatedly over the back of her neck. Every now and then she'd give her head a quick little shake, as if she were trying to joggle some loose piece back into place.

Charles was beginning to get worried. Either this girl had really hurt her head, or else she was slightly crazy. Either way, she was making him more than a little nervous. She wandered across the front of the church and finally came to rest in front of a large statue mounted on a pedestal in the west transept.

The statue showed an angel in armor, two great white wings at his back. In his hand he held a sword, which he was brandishing at a demon he was holding down with his foot. The demon's skin was scaled. His feet were cloven hooves. Two squat black horns thrust from his forehead; two stubby bat wings sprouted from his back. He looked like someone you wouldn't want to meet in a dark alley one day.

The girl stood staring at the statue while he walked over to her.

"Who's that?" she asked.

"St. Michael, I think. Look, maybe you should sit down for a minute. You don't look very well."

She didn't seem to hear. He led her by the arm over to a bench nearby and sat her down. The flickering light from a bank of colored votive lights played across her face. The blood from the cut on her forehead had begun to trickle down her cheek. He fished about in his pockets and came out with a handkerchief, one of his father's. He handed it to her. She looked at it blankly.

"What's this for?"

"The cut on your head; it's bleeding." And when she still didn't seem to get it, he took it from her, wiped the blood from her cheek, and held the handkerchief to her forehead for a minute.

She didn't pull away. She just sat there staring into his eyes. Her skin felt cool to the touch, and her color was off. She was wearing a long faded green coat, several sizes too big for her. It was none too clean, and there was a tear at the elbow of one sleeve. She wore a T-shirt under it. Her pants had a lived-in look about them. On her feet she wore a pair of scuffed black leather boots. The laces had been broken and mended in several places.

He took the hankie away. The bleeding seemed to have stopped. He folded it and handed it to her.

"Thanks," she said, and her face lit up with a little smile that melted him. She looked at the hankie for a minute, then finally pushed it into the back pocket of her pants. She had this very weird way of doing things, as if her head and her body weren't quite connecting properly.

He heard the soft click of the clock on the organ loft. Looking up, he saw that it was after five. He should have left long ago. If he delayed much longer, he would be missed at home. There would be questions – questions he would sooner not have to answer.

"I have to go," he said.

She nodded.

"Is there something I can do for you? Maybe I should find the caretaker and let him know what happened to you."

"No, please don't," she said, and she reached out and took him by the hand. "Promise you won't."

"Promise," he said, after a long pause.

He left her sitting in the shadows and went to fetch his bag from the pew where he'd left it. The noise of traffic trickled through the broken window like the blood from the cut above the girl's eye.

5

He was not dead. Of that much he was sure. Being dead could not be nearly as uncomfortable. Mr. Berkeley lay sprawled awkwardly on his side in the soft soil of the garden. He was lying on something. He thought for a while it might be the ladder, then decided it was far too leafy to be the ladder. He opened his eyes a crack, saw that it was the bleeding heart bush, then closed them again.

He felt strangely disconnected, as if he had happened upon this place in his sleep, as if more dreaming might undo the damage.

Once, a lifetime ago, he and a couple of school chums had sat by a stream one summer's night, drinking rice wine. The wine was sweet and cool on the tongue, and they sat there in the warm dark, leaning against a tree, laughing, with the sky all sprayed from end to end with stars. And now and again, one of them would go down to fetch another of the small ice-blue bottles from the stream, till at last, all six of the bottles lay empty on the grass at their feet, and the sky had begun to spin about the tree. And when he tried to walk he found his legs would not work, so he lay down in the long grass. And one of the others took a bottle and tossed it off into the dark, and he heard the muted smash of it in the distance. Opening his eyes, the sky had been strewn with shattered glass.

As he lay there now, the memory of that bottle breaking merged with the breaking of the window. For the window had broken. He had heard the crash of it as he was falling. He slowly extricated himself from the bush and got to his feet. There was a pain in his right hip and a bump the size of an egg on the back of his head. Otherwise, he seemed to be in one piece. The window had not fared as well.

He glanced up to where the ladder had broken through the glass. The window consisted of six panels. The four central panels were given over to the principal subject; the upper and lower panels served as a border and were devoted to separate, smaller images set in medallions. The entire bottom panel of the St. Francis window had been pushed in. For the first time in well over a hundred years, light passed freely through the opening.

He glanced over at the houses across the street to see if anyone had seen him fall. But the porches were empty, the windows devoid of faces. No one had witnessed his humiliation.

The wash bucket lay overturned in the garden. The water had soaked into the soil. Only the suds remained, like some strange new growth bubbling up from below. He picked up the bucket and walked haltingly along the path that led to the side entrance of the church. He winced as he made his way slowly down the basement stairs and along the darkened hallway to the utility room.

He ran cold water in the sink, wet a clean rag, and held it to the bump on the back of his head. He fetched a broom and a dustpan, and found a small cardboard box. When he had delayed the inevitable for as long as he possibly could, he finally made his way back up the stairs to survey the damage.

As he opened the door at the front of the nave, he caught sight of a boy on his way out the rear. The boy turned to look at him, and he recognized him as the lad who had been coming Friday afternoons. They had nodded once or twice, but had not yet exchanged words. He wondered if the boy had seen the accident, but while he debated whether or not he should speak to him, the boy disappeared out the door.

He made his way down the side aisle to the broken window. The leaden frame of the bottom panel still stood in the window opening along with a few loose shards of glass, but the rest of the glass and the leading lay strewn on the bench and the floor beneath it. He began to gather up the pieces. The glass was of fine quality, much thicker than machine-made glass, textured to the touch, the edges looking as though they had been nibbled down to fit the narrow channel of the leading. If there had been any doubt before that this was ancient glass, there could be none now.

As he gathered up the pieces, examining each in turn, he soon noticed something quite remarkable. One would expect that if a window such as this were to fall, the glass would shatter and the window be irreparably damaged.

But this was not the case. For while the window had certainly broken, it seemed that each of the separate pieces that had gone into composing the design had itself remained intact. Only the pattern had come apart, so that what he was left with was a puzzle in glass. He considered it something of a miracle.

Once he'd gathered all the glass and bits of broken leading into the box, he removed the frame, measured the window opening, cut a piece of plywood to cover the hole, and shimmed it into place.

At the back of the church St. Bart stood with his skin draped over his arm, silently surveying the scene.

6

Charles walked quickly along the street, passing bargain shops, secondhand stores, seedy restaurants with sun-bleached signs propped in their windows, a used-car dealership whose plastic streamers fluttered listlessly in the breeze.

It felt strange to be in the midst of the city again, the quiet of St. Bart's traded for the din of rush hour traffic. He felt his senses assaulted. Daylight seemed too bright after the muted light of the old windows; billboards and bus shelter ads, too brash after the images in plaster and glass. He felt jarred by the experience, as though he had been hurled headlong from one time into another.

That other time was still, almost unmoving. Only the soft click of the clock on the face of the organ loft disturbed the stillness there. Here, cars flew past at a furious pace. Incense of exhaust fumes filled the air.

He tried to set his mind on arriving home, ready to field questions about the mythical piano lesson that would allow him to somehow skirt the truth without actually landing him in a lie. But try as he might, his thoughts kept returning to the girl he'd left in the church. What would happen to her? Where would she go? What would she do? She'd seemed so totally lost.

The caretaker was bound to find her, he told himself. He would take care of her. But the girl had seemed anxious to avoid the caretaker. Still, what was the worst that could happen to her? She'd leave the church, maybe sleep out in the park across the street. She could always panhandle for a bit of cash to get something to eat. She was probably used to that; she had obviously lived on the street for a while. Some kids just like living like that, he told himself. It wasn't such a bad life really, nobody telling you what to do, where to go. There was no point in feeling sorry for her. She wouldn't want his pity anyway. Besides, the cut didn't look that bad. And maybe she was just as weird before the window fell on her.

And then the image of the girl's confused, vaguely frightened face would loom up in his mind and, instantly, all his well-constructed reasonings would be leveled like a house of cards.

It was 5:45 by the clock above the door of the bank on the corner by the time he reached his street. Actually, it wasn't a bank anymore. The bank had died a couple of years back. The insides had been gutted and it had sat empty for a long while. Last winter, the owner of the fruit and vegetable store on the opposite corner had bought the building. This spring, it had been reborn as a gardening center.

Rows of plants in plastic flats were ranged down one side of the building. Bags of peat moss, files of fruit tree saplings, pots of rosebushes, down the other. A mountain of topsoil had been dumped in what had once been the bank employees' parking lot. Despite it all, it still looked like a bank in a bad disguise.

Inside the front window, the owner's wife sat at a cash register looking lonely. There was no one around. The place should have been packed. It was the beginning of the Victoria Day weekend, a time in Caledon traditionally devoted to setting out the garden for the summer. But it had been an unseasonably cold spring. The forsythia behind the house was still in flower; the fruit trees along the street were still holding their bloom.

The days had been cloudy and cool, and at night the temperature had dropped to near freezing. It was still too risky to plant the less hardy plants. Besides, no one felt much like doing their spring planting all bundled up in sweaters and windbreakers.

Gran called it uncanny. She attributed the strangeness of the weather to the automobile. She was inclined to attribute a lot of problems to the automobile. She always called it that, too – automobile, as if it were a new and somewhat suspect invention.

Gran didn't have much use for most machines. She called herself a Luddite and was ready to explain exactly what she meant by that if you couldn't get away fast enough. In the two years they'd been living together, the others had worked getting away down to a fine art. He was still a little slow.

He trotted down the street now. It was a short dead-end street, with a high wooden fence at one end. One of the slats in the fence was loose, and if you squeezed through, you found yourself in the weeds by the side of the railroad tracks.

Theirs was the last house on the block before the tracks; it sat aloof, beyond the line of row-houses that ran down either side of the street. When a train went past, you could have sworn it was going straight through the living room. The dishes jittered in the cupboards; pictures went slightly out of whack on the walls. Fine cracks ran down from the corners of the rooms.

In time, you grew used to the passing of the trains. It became second nature, wove its way into the fabric of your being. Gran, who had lived in the house for over fifty years, barely looked up as the trains went by. If one was late, she would grow instinctively restless, and her eyes would stray to the clock.

It was easy now for Charles to see how his father had developed a passion for trains. He had grown up within a stone's throw of trains all his life; his own father had worked for the railroad. His imagination was crisscrossed with tracks. It was only natural that he carried that passion into his adult years. Even now, Charles could not hear a passing train without thinking of his father.

The car, such as it was, was parked out front. The trunk and the rear door on the sidewalk side were open. His brother, Albert, was coming down the walk, carrying a cardboard box almost as big as he was, feeling blindly for the steps.

"Here, let me give you a hand with that."

"Is that you, Charles?"

"Yeah, it's me. Give me that thing before you fall and break your neck."

Albert was the youngest of the brood. Mother was inclined to baby him. At twelve, barely two years younger than Elizabeth and him, Albert wasn't much of a baby anymore and was determined to prove it. Hence, the box, which weighed about half a ton.

Charles stood at the curb, straining under the weight of it, while Albert took his time rearranging some of the stuff that was jammed in the trunk, trying to make room for it. He finally gave up and they squeezed the box into the backseat, which was already crammed with boxes, blankets, and pillows.

They were packing to go up to the cottage. This was the weekend they traditionally went up and opened the place for the season. They would take down the shutters, haul the hose and filter back into the lake and turn on the water, sweep away the spiderwebs and mouse droppings, wash down the cupboards and floors, repair whatever damage the snow had done to the roof, rake up the dead leaves, and generally reclaim the place as theirs. At the end of the day, they would light a bonfire on the beach and toast the summer in again.

When he was growing up, the cottage had been their home away from home in the summer. They used to spend most of their weekends there in June and July, then go up for two solid weeks near the end of August, when Father took his holidays. Last year the place had sat shuttered and empty all summer. This year his mother was determined to reclaim it.

It would just be her and Elizabeth and Albert going. Elizabeth wasn't any too pleased with the prospect of having to leave her friends and head off into the wilderness, as she called it, for the weekend. There was no telephone at the cottage, and a weekend without the phone for Elizabeth was equivalent to a life sentence on Devil's Island for most people.

This year, for the first time, Charles would not be making the trip. Last fall, hard-pressed for cash, he'd responded to a flyer he'd found stapled to a lamppost along the street. The following week he'd begun delivering the *Caledon Daily Examiner*. He would have to be around to deliver his papers this weekend, so he would be staying home with Gran.

Gran could use his help. Her eyesight had been poor for the last few years, and two weeks ago she'd had a cataract operation in an attempt to improve it. It was too early to tell whether the operation had been a success, for the eye was still healing. She was strictly forbidden to stoop or bend or lift anything heavy at all, for fear of bringing on a hemorrhage and possible blindness in that eye. Gran was a fiercely independent woman and it irked her not being able to do things she was used to doing.

Though she would never tell Gran, a large part of the reason Mother was leaving Charles home was so that he could be around to give her a hand with things. She would need help walking to the hairdresser's to have her hair washed for the first time since the operation, and if she was to shop, she would need him to pull the buggy.

Albert, still young enough to be excited about going to the cottage, had already dashed back to the house for another box. As Charles headed up the walk, his eye flitted over the front of the house and settled on the stained glass fanlight over the front window. In the center of it, there was a small medallion of a bluebird sitting on a branch. It stopped him dead in his tracks for a moment, and his thoughts flew back to the girl in the church.

7

"I was beginning to wonder what had happened to you."

His mother was kneeling in the middle of the living room floor, packing things carefully into a cardboard box. His mother packed boxes like other people did Chinese puzzles. She must have found the empty box in the basement. The words DISHES-FRAGILE were scrawled in black marker on the side of it. The writing was his. The mere sight of it instantly opened the whole memory of the move.

It was a memory made of boxes. It had seemed there were never enough boxes. He began to think there were not enough boxes in the entire world to contain their lives. They had collected them from every possible place they could think of: the supermarket, the fruit store, the drugstore, the liquor store. Boxes of all shapes and sizes, in all imaginable conditions.

Every box they brought home had been instantly filled. Near the end, he would walk the strip on garbage night with the wagon in tow, looking for flattened boxes the shopkeepers had put out for the collection.

He had never dreamt they had so much stuff. Bit by bit they had loaded their lives into boxes, labeled them, sealed them, marked the ones that contained breakable things FRAGILE, and underscored the word to catch their notice later. They could have labeled every box FRAGILE.

"Sorry," he said. "I ran into someone on the way home." *True.* He hooked his bag over the newel post at the foot of the stairs, hoping she would let it go at that.

"Really. Who?" She had a list beside her. Every time she fit something into the box, she would stroke it off the list. Mother was the queen of lists. It could drive you crazy sometimes.

"Some girl. I don't know her name." *Still true, but inching toward the edge.*

He came in and flopped down on the couch. The couch had come from the old house. Its upholstery was worn bare in spots and stained, but its claim to fame was that it opened into a bed. It sat across the room from Gran's couch, looking like a poor relation visiting for the weekend.

Gran's couch didn't open into a bed. It had lion's paw legs, and beneath its ever-present throw, its brocade upholstery was untouched by time. His eye fell on the piano against the far wall and he felt a little flutter of unease.

"Someone from school?"

"No, a stranger. She was lost. I was giving her directions." He was treading the very edge of the truth now. One more question and he would have to start winging it.

It was Gran who saved him. "What on earth can be keeping that boy?" she called from the kitchen.

"I'm here, Gran," he called back.

She came into the kitchen doorway, wearing her huge wraparound shades. Since the operation her eye was sensitive to the light, and she wore the dark glasses to protect it. They looked a little funny on her, but you wouldn't dare say that to her. Her hair looked a little funny too. She hadn't been allowed to wash it while the eye healed.

"Dinner will be ready in ten minutes," she said. When Gran spoke, everyone listened.

Mother quickly packed the last couple of things into the box and asked Albert to take it out to the car, and then get ready for dinner. "You'd better go wash up, Charles," she said. "And tell Elizabeth it's time to eat."

It was strange to be living in this house he'd known so well in another way. Even after two years it did not quite feel like home. The pattern of their lives was a thing still finding form.

As with all old houses, it inhabited not simply space, but time. Its dimensions were not merely a matter of measurement, but also of memory.

He knew the house by heart, knew by rote which stair creaked, which rise was slightly higher than the others, and raised his leg instinctively. Strangers to the house would sometimes stumble on that stair, but the landscape of the house was inscribed upon his spirit, and he could walk it with his eyes closed.

He closed them now as he took his bag and started up the stairs. The room directly to the right at the top was Albert's. He ascended the stairs, took two sure steps, and with eyes still closed, reached out and touched the faceted crystal of the doorknob on the first try. An image of the room, not as it was now but as it had been before, leapt into his mind.

It had been Gran's sewing room then, and when he visited the house as a child, he had always been a little afraid of it. For along with the dusty packets of patterns on the shelves and the piles of fabric pieces Gran saved for making quilts, in the far corner of the room stood the headless figure of the dressmaker's form, its clothes all pieced and pinned. He would squeeze his eyes shut as he hurried past, so that he wouldn't see it standing there.

He turned now, touched the smooth dome of the newel post at the head of the stairs, then started walking, eyes still closed, slowly along the hall, setting one foot in front of the other while keeping the image of the hall fixed firmly in his mind's eye, and himself moving through it. He felt the worn pile of the runner underfoot, pictured the winding pattern of roses that ran the length of it.

The first room on the right after Albert's was his mother's. He reached out blindly, touched the knob on the second try, then continued down the hall to Elizabeth's room. He stopped, reached for the doorknob and failed to find it, felt methodically around, but met only air.

"Why do you have to be so weird?"

He opened his eyes. The door was open and Elizabeth was lying across her bed, staring at him. The phone was beside her. She was expecting a call; she was perpetually expecting a call.

"What do you mean by weird?"

"You're kidding, right?"

Although they were twins, Elizabeth had been born four and a half minutes before him, and always considered herself several years older.

Rooms take the shape of the people who inhabit them. Mother's room was spare and ordered; Gran's, a complex pattern of pieces, steeped in time. Elizabeth had set her stamp upon this room. Before they had moved in, it was Aunt Lucy's room. Aunt Lucy was their father's youngest sister and the last of Gran's four children to leave. She was married and had children of her own now, but her childhood had been kept on ice here.

Elizabeth had changed all that. There were posters and magazine pictures taped to the wall, creams and potions massed atop the dresser, clothes flung everywhere. The only trace of Aunt Lucy left now was the spare bed, which had been hers. Elizabeth's idea of cleaning up her room was to pile all the stuff on the spare bed and pull the bedspread up over it. The lump it made looked an awful lot like Aunt Lucy was back.

"Dinner's in five minutes," he said.

He caught sight of his reflection in the mirror on the wall opposite the door. It took him by surprise and, for a moment, he found himself looking at a stranger. The phone rang. Elizabeth snared it in mid-ring.

"Hello? Oh, hi there. Hang on for a sec, will you?" She cupped her hand over the mouthpiece. "Do you mind?"

He wondered whether having mirrors changed the way people thought of themselves. Did the image in the glass become you? Gran had all sorts of superstitions about mirrors: never show a baby itself in the mirror; never look in a mirror in the midst of a thunderstorm; cover the mirrors in the house when someone dies. He remembered the mirror he had broken while they were moving in. It had slipped from his hands as he was carrying it down the cellar stairs, and shattered into countless glistening shards. Gran had discovered him vainly trying to gather up all the pieces. She had carefully swept them up, put them into a paper bag, and taken the bag out behind the shed and buried it to avert the bad luck that would otherwise come upon him. The memory of the mirror breaking made him think of the window in the church. The image of the caretaker gathering up the glass came into his mind, and with it, again, the girl.

"Charles, would you just go, please? And – close – the – door." She was talking to him in that slow, exaggerated way she sometimes did, as if he were new to the language. As he pulled the door closed, he caught the beginning of her conversation.

"Boy, my brother is *so weird*. I swear I don't belong to this family. I must be adopted."

His room was the one at the end of the hall. It had been his father's room as a boy. The first thing he noticed as he came into it now was the clock on the dresser. It was an old windup clock with an irritating tick and an alarm so loud it lifted you several feet up off the bed when it rang. He took it now and tucked it away in the top drawer with the socks and the underwear.

He peeled off his school clothes and pulled on a T-shirt and a pair of pants. He shook out his school pants, hung them on a hanger, hung the hanger in the closet. His eyes wandered the circuit of the room. There were parts of his father here, parts of himself, parts of his sister Emily. The boxes stacked against the wall opposite the bed belonged to her.

On the wall above them was a photo. It was a picture of his grandfather, standing beside an old steam locomotive. He was wearing his work clothes and a cap, for his job at the old Caledon roundhouse had been to service engines such as this, after they finished a long run. He had taken the photo himself. He had positioned the camera, set the timer, then hurried himself into position before the picture was snapped. One of his hands, caught in the midst of motion, had a slight blur to it.

It was only on closer inspection that Charles had noticed something more in the photo – someone sitting in the engine at the controls, the face of a boy glimpsed through the window there. The boy looked astonishingly like him. He still remembered the shock he'd felt when he suddenly realized he was looking into the face of his father.

8

Dinner had been served and the blessing said by the time Elizabeth finally appeared.

"Sorry," she muttered, as she sat down.

Being Friday, it was fish. Salt cod poached in milk, mashed potatoes, peas. Charles watched the fleeting face she made at her meal. He had known the face would come, as he knew that she would now glance up at him. She did; their eyes met, and thought flowed in a wordless stream between them.

It had always been that way with them. By some sure instinct they knew what the other was thinking, feeling; knew if the other was in danger or distress, as if on some primal level the two of them were one. Like that time in the old house when she had fallen while she was climbing in the bushes out back.

He had been in the house playing, when suddenly a sharp pain caught him in the pit of his gut. A chill wave of panic washed over him, and instantly he knew that something had happened to her. He had rushed out into the yard and found her hanging in the lilac bush, suspended on the spike of a broken branch that had pierced her side.

He ran for help. Father fetched a ladder from the garage and lifted her down. He laid her in the long grass, and you could see the white of her intestines pulsing through the wound. Now, years later, there was still a dime-sized circle of skin low on her side that refused to tan in summer. And when the lilac bloomed in spring, a faint echo of panic laced the perfumed air.

As they grew older, the bond between them became burdensome. They grew purposely apart. Still, there were times such as this when he knew exactly what she was thinking, and she knew that he knew.

He ate quietly, narrowing his attention to the crenellated pattern that ran around the rim of his plate, like the battlements that rimmed a castle wall. He made a hollow in the mound of mashed potatoes, filled it with peas, took forkfuls of the two together, flaked away bits of the fish, took small mouthfuls, chewing slowly, feeling warily for bones with the tip of his tongue.

The conversation flowed around him. He had a dread they would probe him further about the piano lesson and he would be forced to lie, and Elizabeth would sense instantly that he was at it. Then:

"How was your piano lesson, Charles?" asked Gran.

"Fine."

"And Miss Henshaw is well?"

"Yes, she's fine too."

"Charles met a girl on the way home," said Mother, a little louder because she was talking to Gran. "She was lost, and he was helping her. That's why he was late."

"Really?" said Elizabeth, probing him with her eyes. "A girl. That's interesting. What did she look like, Charles?"

"I don't know. She was just some girl. Knock it off, Elizabeth."

"Why, Charles, I do believe you're blushing."

"That's enough, Elizabeth," said Mother. She had brought with her to the table her list of things they were to take to the cottage. She kept it by her plate, and now and then would add an item to it that had escaped her notice.

"Did you remember to pack an extra sweater, Albert? It will be chilly at night up there."

Albert mumbled something through a mouthful of food.

"Don't talk with your mouth full, child," said Gran, who despaired of all their manners.

"I'd like to get an early start so that we avoid the holiday traffic," said Mother. "If we leave by eight –"

"Eight?" wailed Elizabeth.

"If we leave by eight, we should get to the cottage before noon and still have most of the day ahead of us to get things in order. But everything needs to be packed tonight. Understood? Then, in the morning, we'll just have to grab a quick bite and leave."

"I don't see why I have to go if Charles doesn't," complained Elizabeth. They'd been down this road several times before, but that wasn't stopping her from starting down it again.

"Charles has his papers to do, or I'm sure he'd love to come along." She didn't bother mentioning the real reason, lest Gran protest that she didn't need anyone to see after her.

Charles broke small bits from his bread and sopped up the salty milk on his plate. As he did so, he slowly revealed the portrait of a woman in profile, painted on the plate. She had a delicate neck, like a dove's. On her head she wore a crown.

The plate had once hung on the dining room wall, until one day a passing train shivered it down, and it had shattered. Once mended, it had joined the pile of mismatched plates among the day-to-day dishes.

When he was a child and the plate was still hanging on the wall, he used to think it was a portrait of his grandmother as a young woman. There was undeniably a slight resemblance: something in the flare of the nostrils, the cut of the hair; something in the quiet dignity of the figure, which even the cracks that now cut across its forehead and neck did nothing to diminish.

The figure was, in fact, the queen as a young woman, and the plate had been made to commemorate her coronation. The queen was a bit of a giggle to most people these days; but Gran, British herself by birth, was still a fan of the old girl.

Close by her chair in the living room, lying on a low shelf, was the coronation album she had put together from articles and photographs clipped from the newspapers and magazines at the time. Among her collection of paperweights was a sulphide, a cameo of the queen sunk in a crystal sphere, commemorating her silver jubilee. No Christmas was complete until Gran had switched on the radio to listen to the queen's address to the Commonwealth.

The year he caught his finger in the clock, the queen had come to Caledon and they had all gone to see her. Crowds had lined the streets along the route of the royal entourage; it happened to pass right along the main street near their house. He and Elizabeth were perched atop a ladder Father had brought from home so they could see. The car had stopped close by, and the queen stepped out. Gran was so excited, she climbed halfway up the ladder herself to see. It was fall and everyone in the neighborhood was buying grapes to make wine for the coming winter. Wasps buzzed dozily about the crates stacked on the sidewalk, while the queen, clutching her little purse, her pillbox hat perched on her head, stopped to watch a grape-crushing demonstration. Two women in peasant costume stood together in a wooden tub, stomping grapes with their feet. No one crushed grapes with their feet anymore. You used a machine. But when the queen came, you put away the machines and did things in the old way.

The queen stood watching the demonstration politely for a few minutes, then one of her handlers touched her lightly on the elbow and, with a smile and a wave to the crowd, she turned and walked back to the car. Gran quickly handed him up her camera and, as the car drove off to the next stop on the way, he snapped a picture from the top of the ladder – the queen, disappearing beneath the shadows of the bridge.

That had been his first and last glimpse of royalty. The next day a picture appeared in the *Caledon Daily Examiner*. It showed the queen, standing with a slightly quizzical expression on her face, watching the grape crushers. Gran had cut it out and pasted it on one of the empty pages at the back of the coronation album. Later, beside it, she pasted the picture he had snapped from the top of the ladder: a sea of heads with a black smudge in the background. If you used your imagination, you could see the queen's gloved hand rising above the smudge as it sped off into the shadows of the bridge. Pasted there at the back of the coronation album, it seemed that the queen had suffered a sad decline. From the golden carriage, horse-drawn through the thronging streets to Westminster Abbey, to a car stop in Caledon to view a grape-crushing demonstration.

He wiped the remains of the milk from his plate with the crust of bread. There were words in Latin written below the portrait, following the arc of the plate, like the words in Latin on the plaque in the church where the patron's heart was sealed in the wall. Dried down to powder by now no doubt. The glue holding the pieces of the plate together had turned brown with the passing of time; the crack ran across the queen's forehead like a trickle of dried blood.

The image of the girl in the church leapt into his mind: her short cropped hair going every which way, her torn coat, the sound of the glass raining down onto the floor when she stood up; the quiet fear he could feel coming from her as she sat there beside him on the bench and he wiped the blood away with his father's handkerchief.

So absorbed was he in these thoughts that he did not hear Mother asking him if he would like more mashed potatoes. She asked him a second time.

"Charles, where are you?" she said.

"Not home, as usual," said Elizabeth.

"If you got knocked on the head, could you forget things?" he asked.

"Oh, is *that* what happened?" said Elizabeth.

"Never mind, Elizabeth," said Mother.

"It would depend on how hard a blow it was," said Gran. "But, certainly, it's quite possible that a blow to the head could cause amnesia."

"How long would it last?"

"Not long, usually. A few minutes, maybe a few hours. There are exceptions, of course. I once read about a woman who one day found herself wandering the aisles in a secondhand bookstore. She had no recollection of who she was, or how she'd happened to get there. No memory at all of her past life. No identification; nothing but the clothes she was wearing, and a small bump on the side of her head."

"And how long did it last? The amnesia, I mean."

"As long as she lived. She never did remember who she'd been, or where she'd come from. It was totally gone, without a trace, forever. It was as though she'd been dropped newborn into the world that day in the bookstore."

9

The basement of St. Bart's was a rabbit warren of winding passageways and small rooms surrounding a central hall with a stage at one end. The hall was seldom used now; stacks of chipped metal chairs were stored behind the red velvet curtains of the stage. Opening off the hall, a large kitchen with cupboards full of dusty dishes stood dark, save for the faint flicker of the pilot light on the great gas stove.

Mr. Berkeley's was one in the nest of rooms along the passageway that led to the boiler room. It was a small room, spare and simple, with a single window set high in the wall. It contained a dresser with an oval mirror mounted over it, a table with two chairs, an iron cot with a wooden trunk at the foot, a floor lamp, and an old wing-back armchair with a horsehair stool. By the bed there was a shelf of books; on the walls, a handful of pictures.

Most of the pictures were old mezzotints of scenes from the Scriptures – the paper rippled with damp beneath the glass, the matting faintly flecked with mildew. He had discovered them stacked against the wall in one of the storage rooms.

Between the print of Adam and Eve walking in the Garden and that of Moses parting the Red Sea, there hung a black-and-white photo of a fine-looking young woman with an open smile and a piercing eye. It was a picture of his late wife, taken shortly after they were wed.

They had met at Canterbury. She had been apprenticed at the same time as he. It was the glass that had brought them together. They had fallen in love with one another as each of them fell in love with the glass. And what had started out as simply a way of making a little money and learning a bit about the craft had ended in altering the course of their lives.

That course had led them in time to Caledon. Who knows how such things happen? They had opened a small stained glass shop in the artists' quarter of town. They worked in the back, lived above, hung glass from the windows and the walls, strung glass from the ceiling of the shop. They were young and foolish; they fed on dreams. By and by the bell above the door began to ring; commissions trickled in. Time passed while they were turned the other way.

And then, when she had scarcely reached her prime, she took ill quite suddenly one summer and died. The world ended for a time.

All that was years ago, but memory made it now. And sometimes, as he sat still in his room with the weight of the great church perched above him, she would come to him in spirit. And when she did, she appeared to him always as she was in the picture that hung there on the wall.

At one end of the table he kept a hotplate, on which he cooked his food. Beside it, placed side by side on the folded towel where he set them to dry, were a plate, a cup and saucer, a knife and fork and spoon. On top of the dresser stood a canister for tea, another for sugar; a stack of paper napkins culled from local restaurants; a row of batteries for his portable radio; a glass ashtray full of change; a magnifying glass; a statue of St. Christopher, carrying the Christ child on his shoulder; a small bit of yellow bone in a glass cylinder.

The bit of bone was a relic – a fragment from the finger of St. Catherine, according to legend and the faded writing on the side of the cylinder. He had discovered it, as well, in one of the storage rooms. He knew it had once been an object of veneration, but usually for him it was no more than a bit of bone encased in glass. He brushed the dust from it once a week.

He took his dinner quietly now. Toast and cheese, and a pot of tea. Now and then he would look down at the box of broken glass and sadly shake his head.

"What will Father Leone say when he gets back and discovers this?" he wondered aloud. Father Leone was out of town leading a retreat and would not be back until Sunday morning. "It will mean my job, and that's certain. And it was all an accident," he lamented to the picture of his wife on the wall. "A terrible accident."

He lit his pipe, took his tea, and settled into his armchair to take solace in the pages of a book. The books on his shelf had all been culled from the glass-fronted bookcases in the little library that opened off the hall. They were old books. Their worn leather bindings were brittle. He held them carefully so that the spines would not crack. As he read, a dry brown dust would sift down onto his lap.

The lives of the saints were his love. They were like fairy tales to him, full of marvels and miracles. He would sit in his chair, under the yellow light of the lamp, and pore over the woodcuts that ornamented the ancient pages. He would run his finger lightly along the words while he read, feeling the faint bite of the type pressed into the page. And soon he would fall beneath the spell of the story, and the walls of the room would melt away.

The lamp above his head became the noonday sun that shone down on the solitary landscape beloved by the desert saints. His chair, with its lace doilies pinned to the arms where the velvet had worn bare, became the little boat that carried St. Brendan and his crew on their adventures. And the pattern in the Persian rug became the fierce creatures of the sea who were stilled by the saint's words, and circled peacefully about the boat.

If a fly buzzed about the room, he would be reminded of St. Colman and the three small creatures who served him: the rooster that woke him at Lauds to pray, the mouse that nibbled lightly at his ear should he fall asleep, and the fly that walked up and down upon the page while he read and, if the saint was called away, would sit quite still on the line where he had stopped reading, and mark the place till he returned.

These figures of legend and lore were flesh and blood to him. He would leave off his reading and feel surrounded by wonders. The veil that divided this world from the world of spirits seemed, at such times, very thin, and in certain places at certain times, a sudden tear might open a passage between the two.

Now and then, as he sat reading, he would glance over at the box beside the table. He wished it were not there, wished with all his heart that the accident had not happened, but happened it had and he must see now if he could mend the window before Father returned.

He tapped out his pipe, put his book by, and began to empty the contents of the box onto the table. He had cut the piece of plywood to cover the window opening; now he cut a piece of cardboard to the same size and set it on the table.

The window was not large – barely two feet square. It was not, he told himself, an impossible task. Some few pieces still clung to the lacework of leading that had remained intact, looking rather like a web dewed with jewels. But once he had laid out all the pieces, his initial optimism waned. For of the over one hundred pieces of various shapes and sizes and colors, some painted and some not, most bore no apparent relation to one another. The pattern was lacking.

He laid out the leads that had remained intact. There was a bit of an outside edge – two corner pieces with matching glass. He laid a sheet of paper upon them, took rubbings of the leads, marked the glass, then stripped away the old leads and cleaned the glass. He set the rubbings down on two corners of the cardboard, but with no notion of whether they were the right two.

He sifted through the glass. There was a face painted on one of the larger pieces. He set that piece down at the center of the square and stared into the still eyes.

"Who are you?" he said.

Several times during the course of the evening, as he worked on the glass puzzle, he thought he heard noises above him in the church. He sometimes fancied that when the church was dark and all was still, the statues woke, stepped down from their pedestals, and strode quietly along the shadowed aisles.

He took his flashlight and made his way along the passage and up the scooped wooden stairs, wincing with the pain in his hip. He switched on a single panel of lights in the nave and had a quick look around. The doors were locked; the stained glass windows slept; the statues stood peacefully in their places. He turned out the lights and made his way back down the stairs.

That night he had a dream. In the dream he seemed again to hear noises overhead, followed now by the faint padding of footsteps on the stairs. At first he imagined it was St. Bart, moving on stone feet about the sleeping church like a watchman on his rounds. But as the footsteps whispered along the passageway and approached the door of his room, he recognized her gait and knew it was her.

There was a pause, then the door swung open, and he knew that if he could but open his eyes he would see his dear one standing there in the doorway. But he could not stir, could not so much as open his eyes a crack.

He sensed her presence moving through the room; felt her pause over the fragments of glass spread out upon the table; sensed her come and stand quietly over him, checking on him as one would check on a sleeping child. He felt her fingertips brush across his forehead like a whisper of wings. And then she was gone.

He woke in the morning with the memory of the dream fresh in his mind, and the aching sense of her presence still eddying about the edges of the room.

10

Gran was a creature of order and routine. She rose at the same time each day, ate the same breakfast, worked her way methodically through her chores in the same worn housedress. At two o'clock, she took her afternoon nap. She lay in her slip in the dark of her room with a mask of cold cream covering her face. At three she rose, washed, powdered her face, fixed her hair, put on her pearl earrings, and dressed for dinner. It was simply the way she did things, and she was not about to change. Between its measured banks, her life ran clear and cool.

Against one wall of the dining room, on slender spindled legs, stood a curio cabinet – a delicate piece of furniture that held delicate objects. The front and sides of the cabinet were of glass; the back was mirrored. It had three shelves full of small ornaments of porcelain and crystal, ivory and silver and jade. Clustered toward the front of the cabinet, where it could be seen to best advantage, was Gran's collection of paperweights. There must have been close to two dozen of them in all.

Each year on the Victoria Day weekend, with the regularity of clockwork, Gran cleaned the curio cabinet. And so, with dinner done, and the dishes washed and put away, and the chaos of packing for the cottage all but over, she took the piece of folded oilcloth from the bureau drawer, spread it over the dining room table, and began the lengthy process of emptying the cabinet.

Charles hovered about for a while, dying to ask her more about memory loss, but fearful of saying too much. All the while they were doing the dishes, he had felt Elizabeth probing him with her eyes, as though he too were a thing of glass, his thoughts ranged on shelves for all to see. Finally, he sought refuge in his room.

His bag lay across the foot of the bed. As he opened it to take out his books, a faint whisper of scent rose in the air – the unmistakable scent of incense. He closed his eyes and breathed it in and was instantly spirited back to St. Bart's. He swore that if he opened his eyes swiftly, he would find the room all pews and pillars, and the girl would be sitting there opposite him on the bench.

He hung the bag on a hook in the closet and closed the door, hoping he might shut the memory away with it.

He went to the window and looked out into the yard. The neighboring yards had all been given over to vegetable gardens. By late summer there would be lush rows of lettuce and spinach, basil and broccoli, onions and garlic; tomato plants heavy with their fruit; bean plants, winding up elaborate webs of string until their leaves made a trembling wall of green between the yards. But now there was only the bare soil, freshly turned, waiting for the winter chill to come out of the ground before the planting began.

Theirs was the only yard still grassed. Deep flower beds bordered the grass on three sides. The green shoots of the perennials spired up from the stubble of brown stalks. Along one side of the property there ran an old wooden fence, eight feet high, the tops of the bare gray boards ragged with age. On the other side of that fence lay the railway right-of-way, a band of wasteland bordering the raised bed of the tracks that ran past the house.

Weeds and wildflowers flourished there, poking their heads through the gaps in the fence, working their way beneath the weathered boards to invade Gran's garden. With some she was ruthless, but others had insinuated their way permanently among the perennials.

Set in the shadows of the fence at the rear of the yard, just beyond the forsythia bush now in bloom, there was an old wooden shed. Its shingled roof was wound with creepers. At one end there was a window covered by a rusty grate; at the other, a door. A pattern of roses had been stenciled on the side. It looked like a little house.

Long ago, when they were small, Gran would sometimes empty it of the gardening tools so that he and Elizabeth might play in it when they visited. Beneath the patchwork of damp boards that formed the floor lurked earwigs and slugs and large black beetles with lacquered shells. The peak of the roof was hung with webs on the inside, and if you brushed against them, a spider would often scurry out of hiding. Their play would be composed of equal parts of delight and terror: delight at the little house, terror at its tenants, harbored all about them there.

Gran tended her plants with the loving care a mother lavishes on her children. All through the summer, she could be found early each morning working her way slowly about the circuit of her small domain – checking for signs of insects and disease, pulling up weeds, deadheading her flowers, tending to the complex patterns of their bloomings.

This room was his small domain, thought Charles, turning from the window. There were parts of it he had planted, parts he had inherited; there were weeds that had worked their way under the boards. Some things lay dormant, apparently dead, but they too would awaken in their turn.

On the far side of the room, pushed away into one corner, was a stack of four large cardboard boxes, capped by a smaller box. The boxes had sat untouched since he'd put them there on the day of the move. They had became part of the landscape of the room – something the eye slid over, as it might slide over anything that habit made invisible.

Now, for the first time in many months, his eye settled on the boxes and he truly saw them there. On the side of each, written in block letters in black marker was one word – EMILY. It was as if the configuration of boxes formed a figure, so that if he squinted his eyes just so, he could imagine his sister leaning there against the wall, looking silently over at him.

Had she been here, he would have asked her what he should do about this girl he had discovered in the church. He would have shared the secret with her, as he had shared other secrets with her over the years. For Emily herself was a creature of secrets.

But she was not here. There was only this pile of boxes he had packed when he dismantled her room for the move. She herself had left long before. He sat lost in thought, his thumb running back and forth along the line of the scar on his baby finger, while the room filled with twilight.

Among the many books that lined the shelves in the basement room, he remembered there had once been an old medical dictionary that Emily had scooped up from a library sale. He could vividly recall lying across her bed, leafing through it with grim fascination, imagining himself the victim of innumerable diseases depicted there. At the front of the book, there was a series of transparencies: a torso of the human body with overlays of the skeletal structure, the lymphatic system, the circulation of the blood, the vital organs, the intricate network of nerves. He would lie there looking down through the layered figure, awed by the sudden realization that beneath the smooth circumference of his own skin, this same hidden creature pulsed and beat. Who had shaped these overlapping layers of him? Who had spun these dizzying pathways?

For days, weeks, afterward he saw the world with altered eyes, awakened suddenly to the inwardness in things. You walked the surface, but beneath the brittle shell lay the intricate labyrinth. You hung about the doorway, but past the threshold lurked a wealth of unsuspected rooms and winding passageways.

He had felt that way always about Emily, that beneath the surface some mystery moved, that through the guarded threshold same intricate maze wound down to the center of her.

"Emily," he whispered aloud to the still room, as if speaking her name might summon her spirit.

He stood for a long while before the pile of boxes, wondering if perhaps that medical dictionary might be somewhere among these things of hers he had packed away; wondering if it might say something about the loss of memory; wondering most of all if he had the strength to confront the task.

At last he reached up and lifted the top box down.

11

As he tore away the strip of tape that sealed the box and lifted the flaps, it was as if a host of spirits flew free and whirled about the room. The sound of their wings was like the quiet rustling of pages, and their faces were like the faces that peered from the colored prints in old books.

He sat on the braided rug that covered the floor of the room, removing book after book from the box. There were paperback books, clothbound books, library discards, books that had been read into disrepair, books that smelled of basements, books that smelled of age. Books with pages turned down at the corners, books with bits of paper marking some long lost place. There were books of poetry, children's books, books of lore and legend, fairy tales, folktales, old novels with tattered covers, ghost stories, mysteries, books of philosophy and religion. Book after book, box after box.

And not only books, but pictures. Pictures clipped from magazines, postcard reproductions of paintings, photos of famous artists and writers, prayer cards, pastel pictures of saints, family shots, collages, brief quotations printed on index cards in Emily's hand. All of them with bits of dried tape clinging to the back, for they had all come from the walls of Emily's room. He had packed them all himself – taken the books from the shelves, carefully removed the pictures from the walls, packed them all in boxes, sealed each with tape, and written her name on the side. He had carried them up to the corner of this room and there, until this night, they had sat. As the unearthed piles of books and papers lay strewn about him now, he began to glimpse in fragments a room he had almost forgotten.

There was no sign of the medical dictionary he had been looking for, but when he opened the bottom box, under a pile of papers covered in Emily's indecipherable scrawl, he came upon a book that struck a clear chord of memory inside him. It was an old oversized hardcover book. The boards were loose, the binding frayed. The title was tooled on the cover: *A Wonder Book of Tales for Boys and Girls.*

He remembered the book from a long way back. Emily had read it to Elizabeth and him when they were little. Mother had rarely had time to read to them; she was much too busy trying to make it from one end of the day to the other with a houseful of children, and Albert just a baby. It was to Emily that the task fell, and this was among the first of the books she had shared with them.

Holding it now, he had a sudden vivid sense of her presence, flowing secretly through these things she had left behind, animating them, binding up the broken bits into one.

He reached out and traced with his finger the impress of the letters of the title on the cover. It was like walking a winding path, a path he had wound with child's fingers once. He began to leaf through the book. The ornamented type, the brooding woodcuts, the colored plates with their tissue covers – all these woke memory at every turn. There were fairy tales, myths of gods and goddesses, tales of quest and conquest, stories of demons and dragons and the dangerous journeys of heroes.

As he turned the pages, he could picture himself lying across the bed in her basement room, sitting on a blanket in the sun, huddling on a windy bench in the park while she read to him. Everywhere in the book there were rumors of her. Old bus transfers, bits of torn paper, scraps of candy wrapper marking favorite stories. Here, a passage underlined; there, a note penciled in the margin. Brittle flowers with their fragile blooms pressed between the pages; a lock of baby hair tied with a bit of ribbon; a photo of the four children sitting together on a deck chair, with a backdrop of beach and the lake like glass beyond – Emily with a big straw hat on her head, he and Elizabeth looking bony in their bathing suits, baby Albert sitting on Emily's lap, clutching his pail and shovel. A memento of Lake Scugog and those endless summer days at the cottage – days filled with the rhythmic lapping of the waves against the shore, the feel of the warm sun on their bare skin, the long lazy hours spent walking along the shore, picking shells and pebbles from the sand.

It was the juddering of the window in the wind that brought him back. He was sitting on the floor, leaning against the bed, the book open on his lap. It had grown too dark to read, and he was suddenly aware that he had been wandering inwardly in regions he had not visited for a long while.

Before he climbed into bed, he wound the clock, pulled out the alarm stem, and laid it back on its bed of socks and underwear in the dresser drawer. Sleep came slowly; he lay listening to the old house settling about him. He was still awake when a train came by near midnight, rattling the window as it rushed past in the dark, car after endless car.

His thoughts kept going back to the girl in the church. He wondered where she was now. With St. Bart's locked for the night, he pictured her huddled on a bench in the park across the street from it, hearing the same train pass in the night. As the last car passed and the train faded into the distance, he imagined it drawing them with it into the land of dreams.

II

The *Four Quartets* Clock

12

The glass painter dipped his brush in the pigment and stood back to study the picture in glass spread out upon the whitewashed table before him. It was to be a window for a church, one in a set of two commissioned by the parish of St. Catherine's in the county of Norwich. His daughter was working on the other at a neighboring table in the small, cluttered shop.

In another corner an apprentice was cutting glass for the latrine at the local cloth merchant's house. The windows of the shop were open to let in the spring air. The cries of hawkers, the rumble of carts, the scent of lilac and dung drifted into the shop.

The glass painter ran his brush with quick, sure strokes across a section of the glass, detailing a fold in the gown of the figure. The form of the figure itself was composed entirely of colored glass. It was only the finer work that wanted painting.

The design for the window had come from the pattern book bequeathed to him by his father, himself a glass painter – as had been his father before him, who had worked on the windows of the great cathedral of Canterbury. Each in their turn had added their own designs to the book, then passed it down.

He watched his daughter leading up the other window, cutting the soft lead cames and molding them to each piece, tapping each piece firmly home to the heart of the lead, holding the pattern tight with nails as she worked. She was a skilled worker, and his heir. He wondered if she would carry on the craft. It was not unheard of for a woman to do so. He knew of a glass painter whose widow had taken over the shop when he died. It was rumored that in France there were several women painting windows.

He dipped the brush into the pigment again. There was only the face of the figure to do now. He thought of the work his father had done, and his father before him – none of it signed, no trace in the windows of the craftsmen who had made them. He watched his daughter bending over her work. The sun through the window cast her profile in sharp relief. With a few sure strokes of the brush, he captured her likeness in the glass. It would stand as her signature there, the sign of her passing.

He called her over and showed it to her. She looked at the figure in the glass and smiled.

"It's me," she said.

"A memento of you," he said, smiling. "Perhaps one day you'll chance to visit the little church where this will hang and see yourself as you look this day, up there in the glass."

Later, they would fire the glass in the kiln to fix the pigment to it. And then she would lead up this window as well, while he worked with the boy on making the packing cases. They would line them with hay and straw, then lay the windows in and nail them shut.

They would be hauled downriver by barge, then carried by cart to St. Catherine's, where he would see them set at last in the light.

13

He was five years old. It was spring, a sunny Saturday, and the whole family had trooped off to Howard Park to see the spring flowers. He and Elizabeth had brought their tricycles. Gran had come along as well. Howard Park was one of her favorite places.

The park formed a circle. The central area was mown and manicured, but the circumference was wooded and wild. Here, there were oak trees hundreds of years old, wildflowers, and prairie grasses – the last remnant of the oak woodlands that had covered the entire area when the first settlers arrived in Caledon.

All this was of as little interest to his five-year-old self as the crocuses and tulips that opened by the path, or the first flush of bloom on the crab apple trees. It was the zoo he wanted to see. For tucked down in a steep hollow, at the south end of the park, there was a small zoo. There the road dipped steeply down. Flanking it to either side stood paddocks housing mountain goats and musk oxen and Barbary sheep, buffalo and deer and llamas, and peacocks that would sometimes spread their tails in magnificent display.

He could smell the rich scent of damp soil in the air as they slowly made their way along the path by the road, Gran pausing time and again to admire some small flower and name its name. He and Elizabeth had raced on ahead of the others and suddenly found themselves at the crest of the hill that swept down through the zoo.

Father shouted for them to wait there, for the hill was far too steep to tricycle down by themselves. So there they sat, poised at the top of the hill, waiting patiently while they watched the people milling about the pens, pushing carrot tops and celery stalks through the fence to feed the animals.

A popcorn cart, hung with balloons, had started up the hill toward them, its high thin whistle threading through the air. He wondered whether there were candy apples, wondered whether Father would buy them one. He glanced impatiently behind and saw Father still guiding Gran along the path.

Suddenly there was a loud crash – the sound of breaking glass. He swung about, startled, and his feet came off the ground. The tricycle began to roll. As he fought to stop it, he glanced in panic down the hill and his eyes fastened on the figure of a boy standing halfway down, staring back at him.

At first he thought he could stop it, but despite all he did, the tricycle began to pick up speed. His feet came off the pedals, which began to whip furiously around as the tricycle raced down the hill. Terror froze his hands to the handlebars. He tried to steer, but as it gathered speed, the tricycle assumed a will of its own.

There were plenty of people around, but none of them tried to stop him. They simply stepped out of the way and watched as he whizzed by. The popcorn cart loomed up ahead – there was no way of avoiding it; they were going to collide. At the last instant, the tricycle suddenly swerved as though it had hit a stone in the road. The handlebars were wrenched from his grip. He went flying over the top and landed in a heap on the grass verge by the road.

He lay there stunned, his heart pounding in his chest, his cheek pressed against the wet grass; and it was as if time had stopped and an enormous silence had settled over all. He drifted on that silence as a leaf drifts on the surface of a pool.

Suddenly, from a long way off, an alarm sounded, like the shrill wail of an ambulance. It grew louder and louder, shattering the silence, shattering the dream.

Charles sprang from the bed, jettisoned across the room by some force deeper than consciousness. He pulled open the dresser drawer, fumbled for the clock, and finally shut off the alarm. He stood with his eyes shut, resting his head against the open drawer, while the startled pounding of his heart subsided. So vividly had the dream recaptured that childhood incident that the coppery taste of blood from the fall still lingered in his mouth. Finally his heartbeat began to settle; the dream began to fade; and he opened his eyes on the outer world.

It was 6:20. He set the clock on the top of the dresser. It seemed glad to be free of the underwear drawer and ticked contentedly away while he pulled on a pair of pants and rummaged about in the drawer for a pair of socks.

He parted the curtain to see what the day had in store. A thick mist lay over all – the near branches of the plum tree that grew close by the house seemed to poke through it, as if through a thick web that had been spun over the world. A dim halo of light in the distance was a signal light along the tracks. The tracks themselves were wound into the web of mist.

He scooped some change from the saucer on top of the dresser, then opened his door and crept quietly down the hall. He kept to the edges, where there were fewer creaks, so as not to disturb those still wound in sleep behind their closed doors. He tiptoed down the stairs. When he flicked on the kitchen light, there was a furtive scurrying. As theirs was the last house on the street before the ribbon of wilderness that ran alongside the tracks, they had accommodated themselves to the company of field mice.

There was a faint smell of gas in the air from the old gas stove Gran refused to part with. Her room was right next to the kitchen. He moved quietly about, so as not to disturb her. If you took her word for it, she slept lightly, if at all. "Sleep, if that's what you'd like to call it," she'd say.

He poured himself a glass of juice, then threw a few things into a bag: the end of a French stick of bread, a piece of cheese, some leftover date squares wrapped in tinfoil from on top of the fridge.

As he pulled on his jacket, he glanced up at the clock. It hadn't started out life as a clock. Actually, it had started out as a record. It was a long story.

He went out onto the back porch, lifted the old bundle buggy down from its hook, and slipped outside, easing the door closed behind him.

14

He made his way along the mist-enshrouded street, pulling the buggy behind him. The paper drop was several blocks away. He didn't always take the buggy. It belonged to Gran and she tended to be very protective of it. So when he borrowed it, he tried to spirit it away quietly and return it to its hook without her knowing. And all the while he was using it, he was worried that something might happen to it. The old thing was on its last legs; the wheels creaked and wobbled, and the wire frame rattled like a bag of bones every time you went over a bump.

He felt cocooned by the mist. He could barely see halfway down the block. There was no one else around. You could smell the spring – a smell of damp soil laced with leaf mold, a smell of Nature wakening after winter. He had switched from his warm coat to his windbreaker last week. It felt a little chilly now, but once the sun came up the mist would burn off, and it would warm up quickly. He walked half asleep through the sleeping streets, the creaking of the buggy the only sound breaking the stillness. *Sleep, sleep, sleep,* it seemed to say, in a voice unnervingly like Gran's.

The thought of Gran put him in mind again of the *Four Quartets* clock. Like everything in the old house, it had a story – but this one involved him.

It began about a year ago with a school project. The shop teacher came up with the idea of making a clock. The school would provide the battery-operated works and the hands of the clock; the students would work on the disk that was to serve as the face of the clock. You could either make it out of wood in the shop, or you could use an old LP record. Everyone was throwing records away by the binful. You couldn't give records away. People were in such a tear to switch to the latest technology that they just trashed their entire record collections. Gran predictably called it madness. She had a large collection of ancient records. Charles knew it would be utterly useless to ask her to part with one of them. Anything he chose would be greeted with waves of protest, and then she would play it for him just to prove her point. He swore she never threw anything out. She had books of matches going back fifty years.

So one day, when she was out at the eye doctor's for an appointment, he quietly went through the whole record collection. And there, languishing away at the very back of the record box, he found an old record in a ragged sleeve. It looked as though it hadn't been played in years. It didn't even have a cover. The record label read

THE FOUR QUARTETS, READ BY T. S. ELIOT, whatever that was. He even put it on the record player to try it out. It was every bit as boring as it sounded. No music, nothing. Just this old guy with an English accent reading some poem through the hiss and pop of the old recording and sounding as if he was about to fall asleep. No one would possibly miss this record. He was sure of it.

So he took it to school, glued the battery case on the back, fed the spindle through the hole in the center, attached the hands, glued the numbers on around the edge, stuck a mounting hook on the back, and there you were – a record clock. He decided to give it to his mother for her birthday. He wrapped it in tissue paper and wound it with a piece of red ribbon he found. She opened it – and looked at it blankly for a moment.

"It's a clock," Charles explained. "I made it at school."

"It's very . . . interesting," she said. She had to look hard for the last word. She didn't seem all that thrilled with it, really.

Up till this point, Gran had been sitting sunk in her chair in the corner of the room, glancing up from time to time over the top of her knitting. Gran was always knitting; a continuous stream of socks and sweaters flowed from the ends of her needles. She caught sight of the record. The clacking of the needles stopped instantly. She set the knitting down on the arm of her chair and came over to take a closer look.

There was nothing he could do, really; he just sat there and hoped against hope that she wouldn't look too closely at what the record was. It was the first thing she looked at.

"Oh, no, not the *Quartets*," she gasped. She put a hand to her heart. Gran could be very dramatic when she'd a mind to. She could have been in theater.

"Not the what?" said his mother.

"Oh, Charles," said Gran, "how could you have? Do you have any idea where that record came from? It was one of the first records. . . ."

The trouble was that everything in the house was of intense significance to Gran. The whole place was saturated with significance. Nothing was simply what it was. Even a scratched old record at the back of a forgotten box was steeped in meaning. He felt as if he'd just chucked her coronation album out into the street.

It took Gran a long time to forgive him. Even now, she would often sigh pointedly when she looked up at the kitchen clock.

As reparation for the loss of the record, he'd been obliged to sit and read the poem to her in sections over several nights from beginning to end. It was about the most boring thing he'd ever done in his life, but Gran just lapped it up.

Every now and then a line would leap out at him, or Gran would start reciting some passage along with him from memory. Sometimes she'd stop him and get him to go back and read a bit she liked over again. This was before she'd had her operation and her eyes were none too good. When she read herself, she usually used a magnifying glass. There were half a dozen magnifying glasses of various sorts and sizes lying around the house, dust settling on their mysterious surfaces. That day, years back, he'd sat at the foot of the porch steps one summer morning and burned the hole in the back of the *Wonder Book*, the stream of smoke rising like incense in the air. The burn burrowing down into the book. Memory.

Gran's hearing was none too good either, but that was another story. You did well not to talk about it anywhere near her.

"There's nothing wrong with my hearing," she would say. "It's simply that you young people insist on mumbling."

Actually, she had what you might call selective hearing loss – she failed to hear what she didn't want to hear, and heard perfectly every whisper that she wasn't meant to hear. According to her, it wasn't so much that she didn't hear sometimes; it was that she was inwardly occupied. Inwardly occupied. She had a way with words, Gran.

Some months after they'd hung the clock on the kitchen wall, the numbers began to come loose. They didn't actually fall off; they just began to list a little. The six slid over on its side; the one in the twelve leaned over until it rested against the two; the nine drifted down toward the eight. It looked as though the bunch of them had gotten into the brandy bottle shelved high in the cupboard next to the clock.

The odd thing was that while everyone complained about the clock falling apart, Gran actually seemed to prefer it that way. One day she got out a bottle of epoxy and quietly reglued the numbers so that they were all slightly warped. The numbers weren't the only thing that was slightly warped.

15

The bundles sat on the street corner – two of them, wrapped in brown paper, bound with wire. He set to work, cutting the wire with the wire cutter, tossing it along with the crumpled wrappers into the bottom of the buggy. He set the papers in two piles, took one off the top of the first pile, fanned it open to its center, slid the insert from the second pile in, then set it aside and went on to the next. By the time he'd finished, he had a large stack of newspapers on the sidewalk beside him.

He loaded them into the buggy. There was a cardboard box fitted to the inside of it. The box had survived snow and mud and rain. In the process, it had molded itself inseparably to the frame. The words on the side of it were barely legible now. GRADE A EGGS. FRAGILE, they read.

Weekdays, he usually carried the papers in a canvas bag, but on the weekends, with the inserts, they were too heavy to carry. He made his way now down the darkened street, leaving the buggy sitting on the sidewalk while he darted up and down walks, putting the paper between the doors at one house, under the mat at another, in the mailbox at a third. When he first took the route, he had to carry a list around. He kept it folded in his back pocket and consulted it constantly. By and by he looked at it less and less, so that by the time it had accidentally gone through the washing machine a couple of times and was all but indecipherable, he had managed to learn the route by memory. He could practically do it in his sleep now, and sometimes did.

His mother had not been particularly happy with the idea of his getting up at six in the morning. "Practically the middle of the night," she'd said. "You'll wear yourself out," she'd said. "You'll get sick. Your schoolwork will suffer."

And there had been plenty of times through the long winter when the last thing on earth he felt like doing was leaving the warm refuge of his bed and venturing out into the predawn darkness. There had been plenty of bitterly cold days, plenty of days when his were the first footsteps to break a fresh fall of snow. More than once he'd come home after the delivery and collapsed on his bed for half an hour before dragging himself off to school.

Despite all that, though, he'd come to love this time alone in the world, this sense of solitude in the midst of multitude. He loved the stillness of the city then, like a great beast beautiful in slumber. It was a time out of time.

As he walked the route, the mist began to break up, the streetlights went out, birds stirred in the trees and sang the sun up. He had worked his way in a circle back to the main street. Earlier, all the stores had been closed – steel grates drawn across the entranceways of some, deliveries dropped in darkened doorways.

Now a few places had opened. The smell of coffee wafted through the open door of a restaurant; a shopkeeper was busy setting up his display. Charles walked quickly along the street, pulling the buggy behind him. He had a paper left over. As he walked, he went through the route in his mind, trying to figure out who he had forgotten.

He glanced at his watch. It was twelve o'clock. It had been twelve o'clock for several weeks now, ever since the school trip to the museum. There had been a large lodestone on display in the geology section there, with a sign beside it warning that the magnetic properties of the stone might damage your watch. In the time he'd stood there reading the sign, the damage was already done. The watch had stopped. He felt sick about it. It had been his grandfather's, a gift from the railway for his years of service. Gran had made a present of it to Charles when he began the route. He tapped the face of it now with his finger, hoping it would start up again. But the sweep hand remained motionless.

He gave up and began walking again, bouncing the buggy carelessly off the curbs as he crossed street after street. He was moving quickly, not merely to cover the distance, but to keep himself from considering what he was doing. For he was not heading home; home lay in utterly the opposite direction. He was making his way back again to St. Bart's.

16

Charles looked around in the park across the street, but there was no sign of her there. He tried the door of the church, found it open, and went in. He parked the buggy at the back beside the rack of pamphlets and magazines, under the watchful eye of St. Bart. Someone had set a jar of forsythia at the foot of the statue. A few of the yellow petals had fallen to the floor.

His gaze fell on the square of plywood covering the hole where the window had broken. Save for that and the flowers, all was the same; he might have dreamt the entire incident.

He made his way slowly down the center aisle. The bag of food he had brought from home hung from his hand at his side. Suddenly it seemed incredibly heavy, weighted with far more than the few things it contained. He was not sure why he had come. He only knew that it had been laid upon him that he must come back and see if he could find the girl before he returned home.

But the place seemed empty. There was no sign of her here, either. She must have wandered off again on her own, none the worse for the window having fallen on her. He was absolved then, released. A wave of relief washed over him. The tight knot that had formed in the pit of his stomach slackened.

He was standing at the front of the church now. The bank of votive lights flickered before him. He thought of the woman yesterday, lighting the candles for the dead. He felt in his pocket for some change and, without pausing for thought, walked over and dropped a couple of coins in the metal box. He had never done this before; he was not even sure he believed in such things. He took the taper from the well as he had seen the woman do, touched it to one of the lit candles until it took flame, then lit the last candle in the top row to the right, so that he would know which was his next time he came.

The green glass holding the candle glowed with light. He stood watching the flames dance their rooted dance, and suddenly the ground grew uneven under him. And the candles now were flickering in the damp grass before gravestones. And he was standing in stiff shoes by the yawning ground, watching them. Prayers for the dead, release of the soul from purgatory. He blew the taper out, returned it to the well, and turned from the altar to leave.

And then he saw her. She was sitting in a pew tucked in the far corner of the west transept. It gave him a queer feeling suddenly seeing her there like that. For a moment he couldn't move; then, as he slowly made his way over to her, she looked up and smiled.

"Hi," he said.

"Hi." The guitar was sitting on the bench beside her.

"How are you?"

"Oh, all right, I guess."

"I'm surprised to find you here still."

Silence. Her eyes searching his.

"How's your head?"

"Better, thanks." It did look better. Just a slight seam of dried blood above her left eyebrow.

"Where did you stay last night?"

"Right here."

"But how? Didn't the caretaker kick you out when he was locking up?"

"Someone came and said it was time to leave. But I had nowhere to go, so I hid."

"Where?"

"In there," she said, pointing to the velvet curtain of the confessional. Her hand came to rest on the strings of the guitar. Silence fell between them.

He was trying to figure out a way of offering her the food without insulting her. There was a quiet dignity about her that shone clear through her rumpled hair, her beat-up clothes. She had what Gran would call breeding. You could hear it in the way she spoke: slowly, with a certain formality, wrapping each word in silence as if it were an object apt to break. She had a trace of an accent, though he couldn't place it. He wondered if she'd come from another country.

"Tell me about yesterday," she said.

So he told her about how he'd come to the church to escape the piano lesson; told her about the window breaking and his finding her lying on the bench covered in glass and thinking at first she was dead; told her about her finally coming around, the cut on her forehead, her confusion about where they were, his having to leave.

She listened in silence.

"You don't remember any of this, do you?" he said, with sudden certainty.

She shook her head. "No, not really. I remember you, but I don't remember those first few minutes after the window broke." She made a long pause. "And I don't remember anything before being here. It's as if I've fallen into a strange dream. I know I'll wake up in a while, but for now – I don't know how I got here, where I came from, where I was going. I don't remember *me*."

"What are you going to do?"

"I don't know. Wait, I guess. Sit and wait and hope it starts to come clear. I don't know what else I can do."

She fell silent again. He sat beside her, wondering what to do. His eye traveled around the empty church. The east windows were lit by the morning sun – the expulsion from the Garden, Abraham and Isaac, Jacob wrestling with the angel.

Suddenly, despite all that he'd promised himself, he knew he could not simply leave her here like this. He was not at all sure what to do, but he knew that once the next step was taken, the rest would follow inevitably from it. His hands felt icy, as if they were wrapped around the chill metal handlebars in the dream; and the gnawing in the pit of his stomach was more than hunger.

It struck him that she could not have had anything to eat since sometime before he found her in the church yesterday. The offering he had brought seemed pitifully small.

"You must be hungry," he heard himself say. "Would you like to go for something to eat?"

She didn't answer, and he began to wonder whether he'd simply thought the question and not asked it at all.

Then suddenly she stood up. She picked up the guitar and put it over her shoulder.

"Thank you," she said. "I think I would."

They walked together down the aisle toward the back of the church. As they passed the statue of St. Bart, the neck of the guitar brushed against the forsythia and a few more petals drifted quietly to the floor.

17

As they stepped through the church door, she stopped dead. She stood there wide-eyed, holding the door open with one hand, and he could see the panic in her eyes – panic at the sudden sound of the city after the stillness of the church, at the sheer spectacle of space. He thought for a moment that she was going to turn around and go back in, but she let go of the door at last and followed behind him as he bumped the buggy down the stairs. She came down slowly, tentatively, as though she were negotiating some dangerous rock face rather than a set of stairs.

They started walking along the street. Every little while she'd look back over her shoulder at the church. Soon, all you could see of it was the steeple, rising above the neighboring buildings, etched against the morning sky.

There was a time in the infancy of the city when a traveler approaching Caledon from the north could stand on high ground and see the whole town cloaked by a dense canopy of trees, stretching as far south as the lake, with only the steeple tops thrusting through.

Things had changed. The only trees on the sad stretch of street they were walking now were the spindly saplings that stood rooted in squares of soil cut from the concrete. A hundred years ago, this had been the industrial heart of Caledon. Factories vied for space alongside the rail lines that had brought sudden prosperity to the town. Houses sprang up, neighborhoods flourished. But then the time of the railroad passed. The factories closed their doors, and the once-proud neighborhood became home for those too poor or lost to live elsewhere.

Charles was used to walking here in the afternoon. Then, there was plenty of traffic about, and people on the street. Now, except for the occasional car that drifted past, the place felt like a ghost town. They passed ancient empty factories – the faded remnants of their painted names barely legible on the weathered brick, their doors boarded up, half their darkened windows smashed. Still others razed to the ground, sad heaps of brick and broken glass.

They moved along the dead street silently save for the rhythmic creaking of the buggy's wheels and the shuffle of the girl's boots on the concrete. The ragged cuffs of her pants trailed along the ground; her hands were swallowed up by the sleeves of her coat. She looked like part of the furniture. The startle he'd seen as she stepped through the church door had lodged in her eyes. She clung close to his side as they walked.

They passed darkened storefronts. A beauty salon with sun-bleached photos taped to the inner side of the window, two wigged mannequin heads peering out onto the empty street like petrified figures from a vanished world, a NO APPOINTMENT NECESSARY sign propped between them. A bakery with a mock wedding cake in the window that looked as though it had been sitting there for twenty years – the plastic bride and groom still perched on the top, still poised to dare the narrow plastic bridge that led down to the lower tiers.

Dollar stores, junk stores, used-appliance places, laundromats. Stores gone out of business, their windows covered in newspaper. Patchwork of words and pictures. In another window, a neon hand flashed off and on above a crystal ball. YOUR FORTUNE TOLD. YOUR FUTURE REVEALED. Behind the sign, a sheet was draped in the window. It did not quite cover the opening and, as they walked by, he caught sight of the room beyond – empty save for a bed pushed against a wall, a child curled asleep on the bare mattress.

At the entrance to a narrow alleyway, the girl suddenly stopped. A broken wine bottle lay on the pavement. She stood looking down at the scattered glass as if it were some treasure she'd stumbled on.

He glanced down the alley and saw a narrow slit of sky, a glimpse of skyscrapers in the distance, their tops still swaddled in fog. Unreal city. The girl was still standing over the broken bottle, unmoving.

"What's up?" he asked. "Are you all right?" She didn't seem to hear him. He finally had to give her a little shake.

"What?" she asked, as if she were coming from a long way off.

"Are you okay?"

"Yeah . . . yeah, I'm fine," she said, and they walked on.

They passed a TV repair shop a couple of blocks farther on. The casings of several discarded sets were stacked at curbside for the garbage collection. In the window of the shop, a TV was turned on. The girl's eyes wandered to the images flickering silently behind the glass. Saturday morning cartoons. The memory rose in his mind of him and Elizabeth and Albert flopped in front of the tube in their pajamas, their parents still asleep on the foldaway bed in the room beyond. Albert, just a toddler then, kept going and standing in front of the screen. He didn't know it wasn't real. He thought the cartoon characters could see him if he stood there, could hear him if he talked to them. They had to keep telling him to sit down. Emily, by then, had already tired of the TV. She would periodically bang on the ceiling of her room beneath them and tell them to turn it down.

Gran had no use for television either. Since they'd moved in with her, their television had been banished to the basement of the house. Albert and Elizabeth routinely ventured down there to sit under the open beams on the orphaned furniture from their former life, watching TV. He himself rarely dared the basement stairs. He couldn't bear to be down there, couldn't bear the sight of the rows of labeled boxes stacked against the wall, the smoke-damaged display cases sitting by the furnace. It roused emotions in him he could not explain.

A siren keened in the distance now, like a spirit caught abroad in daylight. He glanced up and saw a solitary figure approaching, bearded, hooded. With each step he took, the figure stooped low and touched the tips of his fingers to the pavement in front of him, as if to assure himself that the ground was solid enough to step upon. He peered out from the shadows of his hood with furtive eyes as they passed, then moved on along the empty street as warily as a climber among crevasses.

How wide the chasm between worlds.

18

They passed several restaurants still closed before they came upon a tired-looking twenty-four-hour place. Painted on the glass, there was a picture of a bluebird flying over a plate of bacon and eggs and a sign that read BREAKFAST SERVED ALL DAY. The view through the window was obscured by a curtain of steam that clung to the inside of the glass, and a row of snake plants that lined the sill. The plants looked as though they'd been there a long time. Their pointed green tongues lolled against the glass. A handwritten sign sat propped against the dirty saucer under one of the pots. PLANTS NOT FOR SALE, it read. Just in case you were getting your hopes up.

Charles peered through a gap in the greenery and caught a dim glimpse of the interior: a long counter, a row of booths along one wall, a sparse scattering of customers.

"How about this place?"

"Fine." She wasn't big on talking, this girl.

The first trick was getting into the place with the bundle buggy. There were two sets of glass doors. You went through the first set, then immediately had to swing to the right and open a second set of doors. Whoever had designed the entranceway hadn't taken Gran's bundle buggy into account. He could have left the buggy on the street; a rusty buggy with a cardboard box fused to the inside would probably be pretty safe sitting there. But if anyone did happen to come along and swipe it, Gran would kill him.

After quite a bit of bumping and contorting, they managed to get themselves through the doors. It was not exactly an unobtrusive entrance. Everyone in the place was alerted to their arrival. A couple sitting in one of the booths craned their necks to take a look. The two at the counter looked up from their coffees. A bleary-eyed waitress, with a pencil tucked behind her ear, looked them up and down and disappeared through a set of swinging doors at the rear.

The silence of the place was broken by the sound of the squeaky wheel as Charles pulled the buggy down the aisle and slid into a booth near the back. The girl lifted the guitar off her shoulder and settled into the seat opposite him. She propped the guitar up on the seat beside her. A muffled clatter of dishes echoed from the kitchen as the waitress reemerged through the swinging doors carrying two plates. The aisle was a little narrow and she had to turn sideways to get by the buggy. She made a little sound with her mouth to show she wasn't happy. The smell of bacon wafted through the air as she went by. She didn't manage as much as a glance in their direction as she squeezed past again on her way back.

She continued giving not so much as a glance in their direction for the next few minutes, while she stood behind the counter feeding dishes to the dishwasher and doing her best to make herself look busy. Finally, Charles got up and went over and asked her for a menu. She thought about that for a couple of minutes while she finished loading the dishwasher and he went back to his seat; then she went over and took a couple of menus from the stack beside the cash and slapped them down in front of them on her way back to the kitchen. This time she banged into the buggy a little on her way by.

He opened the menu and pretended to be looking at it, but he could feel his face burning with embarrassment. Anger took the words printed on the menu and twisted them into a meaningless blur. He glanced over at the girl. She was just sitting there, calmly studying the menu. Sitting face-to-face with her under the unforgiving glare of the fluorescent lights, he suddenly realized just how much in need of a wash she was. And every now and then, a smell would drift across the table that even the pervasive odor of bacon could not mask.

The dishwasher belched steam into the already sodden air as it went through its cycle. Charles went to take off his jacket, then remembered that he was still wearing his pajama top underneath and thought better of it.

His eyes drifted up to the clock. Just past 7:30. His thoughts turned to home. They would be sitting down to breakfast now – buttered toast and hot chocolate. Gran would be shuffling about in her ancient slippers. Elizabeth would still be bitterly complaining about having to go to the cottage. Mother would be glancing up at the clock, eager to be off.

The waitress reappeared, order pad and pencil in hand. "Well, what'll it be?"

"I don't know," he said, and then to the girl, "What would you like?"

"I don't know. Whatever you're having."

By this point the waitress was tapping her pencil against the pad.

"Okay," he said. "Toast and hot chocolate. How's that?"

"Fine."

The waitress didn't bother to write it down. She scooped up the menus and went away. They were left looking at one another across the table. The girl had these eyes that went on and on. You could wander down into them and lose yourself. Most people didn't let you look into their eyes like that, but she had this unnerving way of just staring into space, and sometimes you were the space she was staring into. He looked away.

Charles began fiddling with the glass ashtray on the table, turning it in slow circles on the flecked black tabletop as if it were something needing to be done. He didn't know where to start with her, what to say. It was hard trying to begin a conversation with someone who didn't know who she was. It wasn't the kind of situation you found yourself in every day. He made a couple of stupid comments about the weather, but that petered out pretty quickly. She didn't exactly hold up her end. She just let him talk till he ran out of words and fell back into silence again.

"You really don't remember anything?"

"No."

"Your name, your birthday, your parents' names?"

She shook her head.

"Does the neighborhood look familiar to you?"

"No."

"Do you think you come from Caledon?"

"I don't know."

"Have you checked your pockets? Do you have any ID? Anything?"

The girl began going through her pockets. She came out with the hankie he'd given her yesterday. There was blood on it from the cut on her forehead. She kept going through her pockets, but turned up nothing more.

"That's all," she said, tapping the pockets of her coat. "Oh, wait." She paused, reached into an outside pocket, and came out with a piece of glass, emerald green. She held it up to the light, looked through it, then handed it to him.

"It looks like a piece of glass from the broken window," he said. "You were covered in glass when I found you. This must have slid into your pocket when you sat up."

The piece fit easily into his palm. It was roughly triangular in shape. When you looked at it against the light, you could see bubbles and bits of grit trapped in the glass.

Just then the waitress came back with the toast and hot chocolate. She looked at the bloodstained hankie on the table; she looked at the piece of glass in his hand. She put the stuff down on the table and left in a hurry.

There was a marshmallow floating on top of the hot chocolate. Disgusting. He fished it out with his spoon and dropped it onto the saucer. Lord, he was starving. He put the piece of glass down on the table. Tearing the buttery toast in quarters, he dunked it up and down in the warm cocoa.

The girl watched him as he ate. She picked up a piece of her toast, tore it as she had seen him do, brought the piece partway to her mouth, paused suddenly, then slowly put it back on her plate. She did the same thing with the cocoa – brought it up till it almost touched her lips, then stopped as if suddenly frozen, and put it back down on the table.

The cocoa had spilled a little when the waitress put it down. The girl began playing with the wet ring it had left on the tabletop, going round it with the tip of her finger, drawing out one by one the rays of a sun.

He watched her do all this, watched mesmerized as she shaped the sun from the wet ring on the table between them.

"What's wrong?" he said. "Aren't you hungry? You must be hungry."

She shrugged her shoulders. There was a jukebox mounted on the wall above the table. A very old jukebox. She began flipping through the metal leaves, not really looking at the selections, just flipping through the leaves and liking the sound of them slapping against one another. She was making quite a bit of noise, actually.

"Would you like to hear some music?" he asked.

Her face lit up.

"Okay, what would you like?" He began looking through the selections. It was not good. The music was all about twenty years old. Half of the songs he didn't know, and the half he knew he didn't like. Finally, in desperation, he settled on an Elvis tune. He dropped the quarter in and punched out the code. The machine went through its whirls and clicks, and the music started up, filtering through the restaurant.

But it wasn't the Elvis song. What came through the speakers were the spare, measured strains of the opening aria of Bach's "Goldberg Variations." He flipped back quickly through all the selections on the jukebox. There was not a trace of Bach among the old country and rock-and-roll singers assembled there. Despite that, the Goldberg aria was playing through the speakers.

He looked around, but no one seemed to be paying too much attention. The girl had closed her eyes. She was humming along, swaying in her seat to the music. About halfway through the aria, she suddenly reached over and picked up her guitar. She quickly tuned it, then, with eyes still closed, she began to play along with the music, nailing the tune note for note. She was oblivious to all. While the music played, it was as though she were no longer sitting in this tired restaurant on the edge of nowhere, but was gathered up in ecstasy, freed from all care. It was a wonder to watch her.

By this point she was attracting considerable attention. An old man sitting at the counter hunched over his coffee looked up and turned on his stool to face her. Midway through the second variation, the music on the jukebox began to fade. As it drifted off, Charles thought he caught the dying strains of the Elvis song he had selected.

The girl opened her eyes. It was as if she were coming from a long way away. As she took in her surroundings, her clothes, the rusty buggy sitting beside the booth, you could see the light go out inside her and confusion take its place.

The old man at the counter finished his coffee, reached into his pocket for a tip, slid that under the saucer, then came over to the booth.

"I don't know where you learned to play like that, young lady," he said, "but you've got the gift. You surely do." He put a dollar down on the table and slid it over toward her. Then he tipped his hat, went back and fetched a battered black instrument case from under his stool, and headed for the door.

The waitress came over with the bill. Some guy with a toothpick wedged between his teeth had poked his head through the kitchen doors and was looking in their direction.

"It's time to leave, guys," the waitress said. "You want to settle up and move along right now. We can't have you disturbing the customers."

She put the bill down on the table and waited while Charles went through his pockets. He counted out his dimes and nickels. He'd forgotten about the money he dropped in the box at St. Bart's. He added the dollar the musician had given them to make up the difference. He now had fifty cents to his name.

The girl took the piece of glass and put it in her pocket. She hadn't touched her food. They made their way back through the restaurant and talked the buggy back through the double set of doors.

He hadn't bothered to leave a tip.

19

Mr. Berkeley tapped the top of his soft-boiled egg with the back of his spoon. He picked away the broken bits of shell and placed them in a pile by the base of the eggcup. He lopped off the top of the egg with his spoon and ate it, then sprinkled salt and pepper onto the exposed yolk. He broke his toast into small pieces and dunked them in the runny yolk.

He ate at one corner of the table. The rest of the space had been given over to the scattered bits of glass that were once the stained glass window. They lay there like a broken rainbow. Bits of white and yellow, blue and green, red and purple. The yellow was the yellow of the yolk; the red, the red of sunrise; the purple was the iridescent necks of the pigeons now busily building their nests high under the eaves of the roof; the green, the blissful green of spring, the sweet victory of life over death; the blue, the deep blue of the bounding sky.

As he looked at them, he tried to put away the worry growing in the pit of his stomach – the worry that he might not be able to repair the window before Father Leone returned. Since waking, he had thought of little else but the window, trying to bring the image of it to mind. For until he had the image to guide him, there were only these scattered bits of glass, exquisite glass to be sure, but part of no pattern, making no sense as a larger whole. Mere fragments.

He stood poring over the useless wreckage. Somewhere hidden here was a thing of beauty, an intricate web of glass and lead, a vision spun in the mind of its maker, the delicate orb anchored there. He must recall that vision, and pattern the pieces into it.

He rinsed his dishes in the sink, set them neatly on the folded tea towel to dry – the cup inverted beside the plate, the silverware laid out side by side. Then he set about his chores. It being Saturday, he would need to give the church a good cleaning in preparation for the services tomorrow. He would vacuum the vestibule and the nave, dust and polish the pews, set out the hymnals, change the candles in the sanctuary, check the votive lights. Those that had guttered down would need the old wax to be scooped out with a knife and a new candle dropped in.

He kept the spare candles, along with his cleaning supplies, in the basement storage room. This was the room where everything went that had no real place to go. There were dusty boxes of books left over from the annual rummage sale; clothing racks hung with tangled hangers; a dismantled confessional, which had once stood at the rear of the church; various old signs for church events; several pieces of furniture in need of repair. Presiding over all was the life-sized statue of St. Theresa and another of St. Francis. Changes in church teaching had made devotion to the saints a somewhat suspect affair. So these statues and others, which had once graced the alcoves and the side altars of St. Bart's – the objects of devotion for many a pious soul over the years – found themselves suddenly homeless.

They were now tucked quietly away in the various meeting and storage rooms in the basement of the church. Mr. Berkeley had named each of the rooms after the saint housed there. His was a simple faith and he retained a place in it for the veneration of the saints. It saddened him to see them fallen so far. It was precisely devotions such as his that had prompted the enlightened leaders of the church to take the statues away in the first place. For the veneration of the saints all too readily slid into the veneration of their images, a condition bordering on heresy. But Mr. Berkeley cared little for the finer points of church teaching. It was the sad fate of the statues that concerned him.

He opened the door of the storage room and flicked on the light. St. Theresa stood just inside the door, her head tilted slightly to one side, her bouquet of plaster roses pressed to her breast. On the far side of the room, surrounded by bags of leftover rummage, St. Francis stood with outstretched hand. The tips of two of his fingers had snapped off, but he did not seem concerned. A sparrow had alighted on his shoulder and another on his head. They were eyeing the dusty crumbs in the saint's hand with some interest, but had not yet worked up the nerve to spread their plaster wings and fly down to investigate.

"You've no doubt heard about the window," said Mr. Berkeley to whoever happened to be listening, while he rummaged through the candle box, looking for six that matched. He slid them into his pockets, took the wooden duster down from its hook, and wound the long hose of the vacuum cleaner about his neck like a boa.

"I don't know what I'm going to do. That's sure," he said, as he stooped to pick up the vacuum canister. He left the light on in the storage room for the saints' sake and made his way along the winding hall and up the stairs, limping with his tender hip under the load.

The church was still, the light muted. After the long hours spent in the windowless basement, he could feel his spirit expand, unfold until it reached to the uppermost recesses of the vaulted nave, where a small spider spun its patient web.

He set methodically about his tasks. He replaced the six candles on the altar with those in his pockets. He checked the votive lights. With the point of his pocketknife he scooped out the remains of the wax from those that had guttered down, and dropped new candles in. With the small brass keys he kept on a length of twine attached to his belt loop, he opened the money boxes and emptied their contents into a cloth bag. He made his way down the aisle to the back of the church. He opened the poor box mounted on the pedestal on which St. Bartholomew stood and emptied its meager contents into a second bag. A third box was affixed to the wall beside the magazine racks in the vestibule. With yet another key, he opened that box and emptied it into a third bag.

It was a weighty responsibility, the emptying of the money boxes, and Mr. Berkeley felt the full weight of it. It was because of the money boxes that he had obtained his position in the first place.

Several years back, in broad daylight, a thief had stolen into the empty church and broken into the poor box. It was not the first such instance of vandalism. Some months before that, someone had set fire to the curtain of the confessional at the rear of the church. It was a miracle that the whole place had not gone up in flames.

In the wake of the theft and the fire, and with the church becoming increasingly the refuge of vagrants, the pastor at the time, Father Black, had decided that they must either lock the church doors during the day or hire someone to oversee the place.

At that time, Mr. Berkeley was himself one of the lost souls who sought refuge in the church. In the wake of his wife's recent death, he had felt something shatter inside him, and a long darkness had settled over his soul. He was a broken man adrift in a broken world. He walked the streets endlessly searching for something that seemed irretrievably lost. Days stretched into weeks and weeks melded into months. The face that met him in the mirror was a stranger's.

He took to spending long hours sitting in the empty church. Something in the silence there settled his whirling thoughts. Something in the play of light through the windows restored him. By and by he grew still again.

Then one day he happened to see a notice posted on the bulletin board at the back of the church, requesting applicants for the position of caretaker. He applied for the job and, much to his amazement, was accepted. He suspected the influence of Father Black in the affair, for the old priest had befriended him in the time of his affliction, God rest his soul.

He took the money now and locked it carefully away in the large old safe in the vestry, where the altar wine was kept as well. With the window broken already, he dared not court any further mishap. Father Leone, the new pastor, was nothing like Father Black. Bright and ambitious, fresh from the seminary, his mind ran to reformation and renewal. He liked a nice crisp altar cloth and a well-shaped sermon. Old St. Bart's and its roughcast congregation were something of an embarrassment to him, Mr. Berkeley imagined. He, too, was no doubt something of an embarrassment. He sensed that with Father Leone he stood on shaky ground and would do well to tread carefully.

The vacuum cleaner cord snaked up the shallow steps of the sanctuary, curled across the carpeted floor, and disappeared from view behind the altar, where Mr. Berkeley had plugged it in. The noise of the motor filled the nave as he worked his way slowly down the center aisle. He was glad the church was empty now. He did not like to disturb visitors at their devotions, even if those visitors sat with their belongings bundled in plastic bags around them.

He could not but look with sympathy on the lost souls who flocked to the old church. For he too had been lost, and from here to there, it was not far to fall. His eyes went to the side altar. He thought of the girl he had seen sitting there last evening, and then again first thing this morning after he had opened the doors. Such a lost-looking waif. His heart went out to her. He wondered where she had gone.

20

Every time they passed a place with a clock, Charles' eyes would flash to it. It was after nine. Mother would have left for the cottage with Elizabeth and Albert by now. Gran would be beginning to wonder what was taking him so long to get back home.

The sensible thing to do would be to get this girl someplace where she would be safe, and then get home as quickly as possible. The trouble was, he couldn't bring himself to do it. So he kept on walking, letting her lead the way, hoping that if she just walked for a little while, something would jog her memory and start her on the way to remembering who she was.

They had crossed one of those invisible borders that cut through Caledon. Junk shops and seedy restaurants had given way to delicatessens, bakeries, and fruit and vegetable stores. People were up and about now, busy with their Saturday morning shopping. He could feel their quiet stares as the two of them passed – she shuffling along in her tattered clothes, he pulling the creaking buggy behind him. It was obvious they did not belong. He could tell that people took them as a pair. He wanted to say, "No, we don't go together. I don't know who this girl is. Lord, *she* doesn't even know who she is."

He tried pretending he wasn't really with her. He lagged behind a little and watched her from a distance. She was very unpredictable. He was never quite sure what she might do next. She caught sight of herself in a shop mirror once – and stopped dead. It was as if she'd taken herself by surprise. There was a moment of blank, then a sudden wonder in her eyes. She cocked her head to one side, reached up slowly and raked a hand through her raggedy hair, then wrapped her coat tight about her as if she were trying in some utterly futile way to make it fit.

As she passed the displays in front of fruit and vegetable stores, she would reach out and run her fingers over the textured rinds of oranges, gingerly touch the prickly skins of pineapples, bend down to drink the scent of lemons and mangoes; and the shopkeepers would come scurrying out of their stores to keep an eye on her.

The sun had broken through the mist now and was bathing the street in light. They turned a corner and came upon a place that sold cut flowers and potted plants. The flowers were wrapped in paper cones and bunched into metal buckets, the buckets set side by side on a low wooden stand that ran the width of the shop. It was like stumbling upon a garden sprung magically from the concrete. He stood there with the sun warm on his face, while she went slowly from bucket to bucket, stroking the delicate petals, pressing her nose to the blooms.

An old Chinese man emerged from the dim interior of the shop, carrying a bucket of roses – red roses, yellow roses, white roses rimmed with pink at the petals' tips. She went over to them immediately, as though drawn by a magnet.

"They're beautiful," she said, bending down to them.

"Very beautiful," agreed the old man, smiling as he disappeared back into the shadows of the store.

"Look how lovely they are, Charles." And she wouldn't leave off until he'd come over and smelled them too.

"Well?" she said.

"You're right," he agreed. "They're lovely."

She smiled, and he smiled back. And in that moment he knew that all his feeble attempts to distance himself from her were doomed to fail. He felt for her, felt with her. Strands of sympathy had been spun between them, so that even now, there was more of him in this strange girl with her shabby clothes than in all the proper strangers they passed.

If he had not gone back to St. Bart's this morning, none of this would have happened. The incident yesterday afternoon would simply have receded into memory, taken its quiet place among all the other memories one put away. An unusual memory, perhaps, but still just an incident of surfaces, an empty shell plucked from the beach, to be taken down and dusted now and then.

But he *had* gone back. He had gone back because he had looked into her eyes – and seen himself. That secret part of him that would always be lone and lost itself had reached out and found itself reflected in her.

They were walking straight into the sun; it was really starting to heat up. Sweat formed on his forehead. Now and then he'd reach up and wipe it off on the arm of his jacket. Still, he didn't dream of taking the jacket off.

Most mornings, when the alarm woke him, he'd simply stumble out of bed half-dazed and pull on his pants and socks, as he had today. He'd just put his jacket on over his pajama top while he did the route, then change when he got back home. He found himself wishing he'd changed first today.

It was his favorite pajama top, and he'd worn it threadbare. Every time it went in the wash, his mother threatened to throw it out. It was a pullover top, long sleeved, pale blue with dark blue at the collar and cuffs. The stitching had come out at the shoulder on one side, and the cuffs had begun to fray. There were other tops, of course, folded neatly in the drawer, and now and then he was forced to wear one. But whenever he did, sleep eluded him.

On the front of it, rather faded now, there was a picture of a steam engine, smoke billowing from its stack as it emerged from a tunnel. On the back there was a picture of a caboose, seen from behind as it disappeared into the far side of the tunnel, as if between the two the track passed through inward parts.

It wasn't just the fact that he was wearing his pajamas that bothered him now. It was the picture of the train on the front and back that caused him to keep his jacket on and the zipper done up.

The hotter it got, the more the creaking of the buggy got on his nerves. It was different in the early morning; then the sound was companionship as he threaded the empty echoing streets. In the dead of winter, the tracks of the two of them through the unbroken snow, the pattern of his footprints in the weaving lines of the wheels, had been like notes upon a staff. The music of their moving.

Now, abroad in daylight, there was no music. Only the harsh screech of it, like the crows in the bare branches shrieking at the sun. And the wrappers and wires poking out of the old cardboard box. And him walking about in his nightclothes. One of those things that happens in a dream.

For the first time he thought of ditching the buggy, just ducking down the next alley they came to and leaving it there. He began to walk faster, staring fixedly at the sidewalk, ignoring stares.

What was he going to do? He had delayed and delayed, but he could delay no longer. He either had to head home right away, or else call and make some kind of excuse for why he wasn't there. But what could he say? That he'd been hiding out yesterday at a run-down church while he was skipping his piano lesson; and a window had broken, and a homeless girl had been hit by it and couldn't remember who she was; so he'd gone back this morning to see if she was all right?

His Gran would think either that he was lying, or that he'd gone mad. The second wasn't far off. And on the off chance that she did happen to believe him, the first thing she'd want to do would be to call the police – which was the last thing the girl wanted him to do. So there you were: nowhere.

The sweat was streaming off him now. Every now and then he'd glance back to make sure the girl was still there. What if she was faking it? What if this whole amnesia thing was some elaborate scam? What if she was just some psycho on the run from the law, trying to milk him for everything he had, which was laughably little?

So completely absorbed was his mind in its own turnings that he was oblivious to everything around him. He bumped the buggy down off the sidewalk and started across the street.

There was a screech. He looked up and saw a car heading straight for him, no more than a car's length away. He saw the look of shock on the driver's face, heard the high keen of the brakes, watched the slow swerve of the car as it bore down upon him. And in some incredibly calm spot inside himself, he knew he was going to be hit.

21

Thwack went the handle of the wooden duster as it banged up against the end of the bench. *Thwack!* Mr. Berkeley worked his way steadily from row to row, the sound of the duster echoing rhythmically through the empty church, punctuated now and then by the thud of a kneeler being knocked into place. He gathered up the stray bulletins as he went along, carefully flattening and refolding them. He paired the missals and hymnals and spaced them uniformly in the racks that ran along the back of each bench. *Thwack* went the duster at its work. *Thwack!*

The ritual of cleaning, with its clear rhythms, calmed his thoughts somewhat. He moved slowly from row to row, leaving order in his wake. Would that he could coax such order inward. Still, the outward ordering often served the inward.

He was thankful there was no funeral this morning. Often on a Saturday there was a funeral. For the congregation of

St. Bart's was an aging one, and many a Sunday, sitting in a rear pew wrapped in shadows, Death could be seen running a chill eye over the assembled.

There would be no hiding the broken window, had there been a funeral. And it would be a sad thing for the mourners to see the rough piece of plywood over the window opening. For grief itself was already a wounded thing. And on such a sad day, with the somber strains of the organ echoing through the nave and the dark smell of funeral flowers in the air, brokenness was surely in need of no reminders. *Thwack!*

Often enough there would be hardly a handful of mourners, for those who might have mourned the passing had themselves already passed. Sometimes then he would slip down to his room to fetch his jacket and tie and sit through the service himself to swell the ranks. And be put in mind of those he loved, who themselves had passed. And be put in mind, too, of his own mortality. Not that he was near old. In the middle way, perhaps. Old enough to have begun to perceive the pattern, to know the things that bounded him. But not so old as to feel jaded. Young enough still to be surprised, to expect the miraculous at every turn; the child in him standing on tiptoe to peer out the eyeholes of him. *Thwack!*

But still, when he sat among the mourners and the sad procession passed, something of himself whispered down the aisle on quiet wheels; something of himself lay couched on satin there; something of himself harked when the censer rattled lightly against the chain and the incense crept through the cracks.

Cracked, thought Mr. Berkeley. We are each of us cracked in our own way. The question was whether it was a crack that let in the darkness or the light. Now and then as he worked, he would glance up at the broken window, hoping that somehow time would have been tricked back into the before. Fragments of colored light flecked the benches. As the duster passed silently through them, he thought back to sweeping up the broken glass, to the sound it made being scooped into the dustpan. Who, he wondered, could scoop this scattered light? *Thwack!*

The light through the old windows was quite unlike the light through the windows in the rest of the church. They took sunlight and shattered it into luminous jewels, spilling them down the backs of benches, flinging them carelessly on the floor. The other windows worked nothing like this magic. But it was a quiet magic, and not everyone noticed it. Yet now and then, someone would wander into the church who knew their true value, the history they held, who sensed the infinite care that had been taken in their composition. That one would walk up and stand silently before them, awed by their art.

Sometimes too, on a Sunday during service, he would see someone in the congregation, often a child, transfixed by the play of light. He would watch them study the spill of light on the back of a bench, then look up at the window. And he would feel a secret bond between them, so that when the small hand reached out and ran a finger through the colored light, he could feel his own hand reaching, the light eluding both their grasps – as now the duster swept vainly through the scattered jewels. *Thwack!*

22

There was no time to run, no time to jump – simply time to stand there clutching the bundle buggy, watching the whole thing happen as though in slow motion; feeling this instant of time unfold itself with ease on all sides round like a flower, and himself at the center of its opening.

Charles' thoughts turned to flowers. He thought of flowers bundled, flowers bunched in buckets, ranged in long rows on low wooden stands; he thought of cut flowers wilting in a crystal vase, the rank smell of the water they sat in, the random pattern of fallen petals on the tabletop. Bad luck to bring funeral flowers back home, said Gran. Bad luck to mix the white and red in the one vase. An ill omen to pick up a fallen flower. "Pick up flowers, pick up sickness," she would say.

He saw her stooping in the dream to smell the flowers by the path, felt the awful roll of the wheels under him as the tricycle began to gather speed and sent him hurtling down the hill. And for a moment, he knew with blinding clarity that nothing was ever really forgotten, that all was always now.

All this happened in the space between one heartbeat and the next. And all the while, here was the car coming. And he wondered how he could have been so warm moments before because now he was cold, unimaginably cold, as if suddenly it were the dead of winter again, his bare hand frozen against the chill metal handle of the buggy.

He looked at the driver of the car. He could see her clearly now. Her eyes were locked on his, and he could read the terror there, see her mouth drop open in shock. Then she closed her eyes and, as if it were a kind of cue, he closed his own.

Suddenly there was a sharp jerk on his shoulders and he felt himself being whirled back, felt the buggy being wrenched violently from his grip. He smacked his mouth hard against the concrete as he landed in a heap on the sidewalk. Then the screech of brakes stopped, and in the silence that followed he heard a car door close.

The first thing he saw when he opened his eyes was the girl from the church leaning over him.

"Are you all right?"

"I think so," he said, even as he brought his hand up to his mouth and touched wetness there.

"You cut your lip," she said.

And then the woman from the car was there. "Oh, my God, is he okay? I couldn't stop. He just stepped off the curb. He didn't even look."

"He's all right."

"I'm all right," Charles said, sitting up now, leaning back against a paper box. The first thing his eyes fell on was the bundle buggy wedged between the bumper and the front wheel of the car. His injuries paled before the plight of the buggy. He prayed it would be salvageable. He would be in deep trouble if he'd broken Gran's bundle buggy.

"If you hadn't pulled him back, I don't know what would have happened. I could have killed him. Lord, he just stepped off. He didn't even look. There was nothing I could do. Is he going to be okay? Is he really going to be okay?" The poor woman was frantic.

"I'm all right," he said. "I'm all right," more to calm her down than anything else. He was having a hard time talking right. His mouth felt several sizes too big for him. He realized now that it was the girl who had saved him. The jerk he had felt had been her hauling him back out of the path of the car.

By now a crowd had begun to gather. People asked what had happened, and stood around staring, and he in the midst of them sitting there like a fool on the sidewalk. The girl reached into her pocket and pulled out his hankie. She refolded it to a clean spot, pressed it to his lip, and held it there.

He got to his feet and stood leaning against the paper box. The mystery of the extra paper skittered briefly over the surface of his thoughts again, then sank. People were looking at him as if he were some new life-form just landed from another planet. The driver of the car kept firing questions at him a mile a minute: "Are you feeling faint? Do you want me to drive you to the hospital or something? Do you want a lift home?"

The girl had moved apart from the crowd now. She was leaning against the window of the variety store on the corner. Hanging inside the window there was a clock, part of a sign advertising cigarettes. It was getting on toward ten. All he wanted was to get his bundle buggy and get away from there.

The girl walked over to the car, gave a couple of hard tugs on the buggy, and managed to extricate it from under the bumper. Some of the bars had been bent out of shape. One of the wheels grated against the frame as she pulled it over to him.

"I guess we should be going now," she said, and he nodded.

"But maybe he should see a doctor," said the driver of the car.

"Do you want to see a doctor?" the girl asked him.

"No, I'm fine."

"He's fine," she said and took his arm. They passed through the crowd and began to walk away. He felt a little wobbly. The wheel was really grating. They turned down the next side street. He found a stick in the gutter and they used it to pry the wheel away from the frame. Lord, Gran was going to kill him.

23

He was standing in a phone booth – standing with his quarter in the slot and his finger on the quarter so that it wouldn't drop. He'd been standing there for some time. His courage had taken him as far as lifting the receiver from the cradle and fitting the quarter into the slot, and then it had deserted him.

Every now and then someone would drift up to the booth, peer in at him, then pace about impatiently for a few minutes while he engaged in an animated conversation with the dial tone. Finally, they'd give up and wander off in disgust down the street, looking for another phone. It would not be an easy task. He had tried half a dozen booths and lost a quarter before he found one with a working phone. This one was more than a little ravaged. Some enterprising thief with a taste for pyromania had torn up one of the phone books and lit a fire under the money box. The money box was still intact, but the phone casing looked like a spent candle.

With the sun beating down through the glass, it felt hot enough in the closed booth to melt the phone without the fire. He had finally been forced to swallow his pride and shed his jacket. He'd managed to squirm his way out of it without letting the quarter drop, which must have looked pretty funny to anyone who happened to be watching. It hung now from the arm that held the quarter in place. He looked a little like St. Bart with his skin draped over his arm. There was a bit of blood on the front of it from his smashed lip. The lip was swollen to twice its normal size. It was as hard as a rock. He kept feeling at it with his teeth. He looked like he'd been in a brawl and, with the way it pressed against his upper lip, he couldn't talk properly. His words came out slightly slurred.

The girl was sitting on a bench outside the booth, minding the buggy. The buggy did not so much look like it needed minding as burying. On the corner across the street, there was a funeral parlor. A couple of people in suits were standing outside having a smoke. There was a clock worked into the sign that hung above them. You could always count on a funeral home to have a clock, a little reminder, he imagined, that time was ticking away and your number would soon be up. His was up, right about now.

It was 10:15. His arm was getting tired, he was hot, his lip was throbbing, he was two hours late getting home, and he had ruined Gran's bundle buggy. He went over his story again in his mind; it was a different story than the last one. He had definitely decided that the truth was not an option.

Once you were cut adrift from the truth, the possibilities were endless. Invention ran in several directions simultaneously. The only question was which one Gran would be most likely to believe.

He had worked his way to the very edge of action. He did not look out the window of the booth at the buggy now. He had a superstitious belief that Gran would somehow be able to sense the wounded buggy if he was looking at it while he spoke to her. Instead he concentrated his attention on the quarter in the slot, on his finger on the quarter, on the image of the queen, partially obscured by his finger.

He thought of dinner last night, sopping up the salty milk with bits of bread to uncover the portrait of the young queen. He thought of the plate hanging on the dining room wall and his taking it for a portrait of Gran. He thought of the train rattling past the house one night, the plate shivering down off the wall in the dark. And at that moment, as if in harmony with the memory, he lifted his finger off the quarter and let it drop. He would not have been surprised to hear it shatter. Instead there was a muffled *thunk* and the dial tone grew louder. He dialed the number.

The image of the house came into his mind – the image of Gran in her dark glasses, moving through it. There was something supremely regal about her. It lay far deeper than her superficial resemblance to the queen; it was something in her manner, in her bearing. She had about her the aura of a monarch in exile. Though she had lived in Caledon most of her life, she always considered herself something of a visitor. Her real home would always lie elsewhere.

She had twice been back to England, but failed to find it there. The scenes she remembered from her youth had vanished; in their stead stood a place utterly foreign to her. Time had passed its hand over the landscape she remembered and altered it irrevocably. In the end, England was more foreign to her than Caledon, for being so tauntingly familiar. The world she sought lay somewhere neither boat nor plane could take her. It lay inward, and was made of memory.

He knew pieces of the story. Sitting in her favorite chair, with the photo album open on her lap, she would tell it like a fairy tale. The others had no time to listen, no patience for her painstaking details and endless elaborations. They would make their quiet escape, but he would sit beside her and fall under the spell of the telling with the same ease that he had once fallen under the spell of the stories Emily would read him from the *Wonder Book*.

He would point to one of the pictures in the album, ask her a question, and have her started on a story. She had a wealth of stories, each connected with the other in intricate and surprising ways. She started out in one story and ended up in another. She pulled up one story, and several others came attached, the way the hooks on hangers become caught on one another, so that you reach for one and several come away.

Gran came from money. Coming to Caledon had been something of a descent for her, as she was all too ready to remind you. The time of her childhood had assumed a mythic status in her mind, like the blissful life in Eden before the Fall. There was a picture of the house she had lived in then. It was a large house – all weathered brick and mullioned windows and ancient ivy creeping up the walls. She had been a promising pianist, and life then had been punctuated by elaborate parties at which she always played, by outings on horseback, and by tennis on the clay courts behind the house.

"And then the war came. I was eighteen at the time. Young, full of ideals. So I joined the Women's Army Auxiliary Corps, traded in my fine clothes for a uniform. And instantly I was indistinguishable from all the other girls from all manner of backgrounds. But I loved it – loved the adventure, the daring of it. It was all so different from the life I'd led before. And I felt that I was somehow doing something worthwhile in the midst of those terrible times.

"I was stationed at a camp near an army base, where soldiers were going through final training before being shipped over to Europe to fight. And one day there was a dance, and I went. It was quite unlike the dances I had known – loud and raucous and a fair sight wilder than I was used to. And then my eye fell on this one young man and, as soon as I saw him, I knew I wanted to talk to him; for like me he seemed a little at a loss in the midst of it all, kept a little apart from it as I did.

"He was a fine figure of a man, tall and lean, with a strong clean profile, and hair as dark as a raven's wing. By and by he came over and asked me if I wanted to dance. He was a wonderful dancer, and he'd a sweet voice and a ready smile. He told me he was from Canada. I'd never known a Canadian before; it was something exotic, like a rare bird. We danced all night together, and then we went out and sat under the stars and watched the moon.

"Now and then, the sky would suddenly light up as a German buzz bomb passed overhead en route to some random target in the distance. And suddenly life seemed so brutally short, and the fine things so desperately fragile. We fell quickly in love, knowing next to nothing of one another. There was no time in wartime. Within days his papers came through. Within a week we were married. Within two weeks he was shipped out with his regiment.

"It was two years before the war ended and we saw one another again. In the time between, I'd given birth to our first child – your father, Charles. He was more than a year old when your grandfather first held him.

"And then he was whisked off to Canada with the returning troops, and I was left behind with the baby. It was nearly a year later when I was rounded up – along with all the other war brides – packed into an old troopship, and sent across the sea. I lay sick in my bunk all the way, with the baby sick beside me. It was bitterly cold when we landed in Halifax. Straight from the immigration shed, we were trundled onto waiting trains. Four trains, ten cars in each, all full of war brides and their babies.

"The trains worked their way slowly across the country, stopping at all hours of the day and night to drop women into the waiting arms of husbands they hardly knew. Love sometimes lies. And the tales men told of their lives back home were told in the heat of love. Some women who had lived in cities all their lives found themselves suddenly on rough homesteads on the open prairie, without electricity or running water; others found themselves in small fishing villages clinging to a rocky shore. I found myself in Caledon."

24

She picked up the phone on the fourth ring.

"Hi, Gran. It's Charles. . . . Yes, everything's all right. . . . I'm sorry. I didn't mean to make you worry. . . . I know I should have called. . . . The papers were late . . . yeah, really late. . . . I don't know. Some problem with the presses maybe. . . . Pardon? . . . . I don't know why I sound funny . . . bad connection, I guess."

Lord, he was going to fry for all the lies he was telling. If hell was anything like this phone booth, it was going to be no fun at all. He was sweating like a maniac. He reached up and wiped his face on the arm of his pajama top and, despite his promise, sneaked a peek at the buggy and the girl on the bench.

A baby stroller had appeared since last he looked. It was parked in front of the fruit store opposite the bench. Strapped inside the stroller there was a baby.

The baby looked about a year old. It had lost that totally dazed look that really young babies have, and had graduated to the stage where it was trying to put it all together. It was sitting in the shade under the fringed hood of the stroller, with a rag doll in its hands, looking happily around while it chewed away on the doll's arm. It caught sight of the girl and the bundle buggy, and it stopped its chewing short.

The girl smiled and waved. She uncrossed her legs, leaned forward, and started talking to the baby. Charles couldn't tell what she was saying. The baby sat very still in its stroller and stared at her. It had never met anyone quite like this before in its brief life.

"Sorry, Gran, what did you say? . . . . I'm in a phone booth. Down near the library. I have this project I'm supposed to hand in on Tuesday, so I thought I'd drop by there and . . . I know I should have said something. I didn't think. . . . It's about memory . . . yes, that's why I was asking you about that last night." His mouth hurt; he was slurring his words all over the place.

"Look, Gran, promise me you won't go lifting anything heavy now, and don't stoop. You know what the doctor said. . . . I know I'm supposed to be there to help . . . I know. I can pick that up when I get there. . . . No, promise me you won't try to do that yourself."

He glanced out the window and noticed that the baby had taken the rag doll out of its mouth and was dangling it over the side of the stroller. It looked at the doll, looked at the ground, then dropped the doll for no other reason than to watch it fall. It landed in a heap on the pavement.

That simple act instantly set a complex machinery in motion. Standing tethered to the phone, encased in glass, there was nothing he could do but watch.

"Sorry, Gran. What did you say? . . . . Yes, I took the package of date squares from the top of the fridge . . . I'm sorry, I didn't know it was for them. . . . Yes, I took the buggy too . . . yes, I'll be careful with it . . . I know. I know. . . . No, I haven't forgotten about your appointment at the hairdresser's. . . ."

The doll had no sooner hit the ground than the girl darted off the bench to retrieve it. She had just picked it up and was trying to give it back to the baby, who wanted no part of it, when the mother came bolting out of the store. Even through the glass of the booth, he could hear her loud and clear.

"What do you think you're doing? Get away from my baby! Get away!" The woman was so upset, she dropped her bag. Oranges rolled in all directions over the sidewalk. The baby took one look at the state she was in and started to bawl. The girl tried to comfort the baby; this set the mother into renewed hysterics, which set the baby to bawling even louder. Meanwhile, Gran kept talking, the oranges kept rolling. One came to rest against the wheel of the buggy, a couple settled in the cracks of the sidewalk, several rolled off the edge of the sidewalk onto the curb, one meandered over in his direction, drifted under the door of the booth, and bumped up against his toe.

"Look, Gran, I've got to go. I'll be home as soon as I can, okay? . . . No, everything's just fine. . . . Yes, I'm sure. . . . Look, I have to go. Bye. . . . Bye."

Gran had not been quite ready to say good-bye. As a matter of fact, she was still talking when he hung up the phone. He scooped up the orange at his feet and bolted out of the booth. The mother had stationed herself between the baby and the girl. She was still going on. The girl hadn't said a word all this time. She just stood there, looking dazed and helpless, holding the rag doll in her hand.

Charles tried to intervene. "It's all right," he said, walking over to the mother. "The baby dropped the doll. This girl was just trying to give it back to her."

He held the orange out to the woman. She gave him a long look. Her eyes traveled from his smashed lip to his bloodstained pajama top to the orange in his outstretched hand. It took her about a second to work the whole thing through in her mind. In that time she decided that, whereas before she had thought there was just one of these crazy people, there were in fact two. Charles watched a series of emotions pass over her face: first confusion, then caution, and finally, fear. Even as he stood there holding out the orange to her, she backed off a few steps, in the way you try to ease away from a dangerous dog. She kept her eyes fixed on the two of them as she felt blindly for the brake of the stroller with her foot. She released it and began walking quickly away. She didn't bother with the doll; she didn't bother with the oranges; and she didn't look back once.

Charles stood holding the orange, staring after her as she disappeared down the street. The girl sat back down on the bench, cradling the doll in the crook of her arm.

He looked at her and thought of Gran as a young war bride, holding her baby, his father, in the crook of her arm as she stepped off the train in Caledon.

"It was snowing. More snow than I had ever seen. I stood there on the empty platform with the baby in my arms, while the bags were unloaded from the baggage car. And I felt as if I had just been set down at the very edge of the world. There was no one there to meet us, so I went into the depot and sat shivering on a bench in the waiting room. In a while I heard the approach of a car; the door of the waiting room opened and a figure bundled in a heavy overcoat came in. It was your grandfather. I didn't recognize him at first. I'd never seen him in anything but his uniform. He seemed smaller than I remembered, shrunken. The whole world seemed cold and shrunken.

"He apologized for not having been there to meet us. The car had become stuck in the snow and he had needed help to push it free. He loaded the luggage into the trunk of the car. As he drove cautiously through the snowbound streets, we searched for things to say. We were like strangers to one another.

"Finally he turned down a dead-end street still choked with snow, and there at the end of it was this house, huddled up against a high wooden fence bordering the train tracks. It looked small and pinched and sad, not at all as imagination had painted it. As I walked up the porch steps with the baby, my eye fell on the stained glass fanlight over the front window – that medallion of the bluebird sitting on a blossoming branch. Somehow the sight of it cut me to the heart, and I began to cry.

"All that winter I cried, desperately, hopelessly. Your grandfather must have thought I had lost my mind. I felt like a figure in a fairy tale, swooped away and shut in a cage of ice. I had never dreamt such homesickness possible, such an ache of loss that I thought I might die of it. For months I stayed shut up in the house, while the snow fell and the baby fussed and the trains rumbled past at all hours of the day and night.

"By and by the weather warmed, the snow melted, and spring came. We bought the piano, and I began to play again for the first time since I'd left home. I made my way outside with the baby and I planted our first garden – an English garden – with seeds ordered through the mail-order catalogs, or tucked between the leaves of letters sent from home. Those two things – the piano and the garden – helped bring a bit of home here, and somehow they saved me."

Gran always referred to that first winter as the time of her breakdown. Like the queen who had been shaken down from the wall, she too had been broken and mended, though the cracks showed in quieter ways.

III

Buggywalk

25

In the year 1547, by force of Royal Injunction, Edward VI ordered the churches of England to "take away, utterly extinct and destroy all shrines, coverings of shrines . . . pictures, paintings, and all other monuments of feigned miracles, pilgrimages, idolatry, and superstition: so that there remains no memory of the same in walls, glass-windows, or elsewhere. . . ."

In the wake of this Injunction, the stained glass windows in churches throughout the country were either willingly removed or forcibly battered down, the leading melted down, the glass dumped in the town ditches.

Some few were saved by being taken down and hidden. Such was the case at the small country church of St. Catherine in the county of Norwich. Under cover of night, the windows were quietly removed and hidden away in a hollow beneath the floorboards of the rectory barn. There they were safely stored during the cycles of destruction, which went on intermittently for well over a hundred years. In time they were completely forgotten, and the years rolled over them.

In the 1830s the railroad came to Norwich. To make room for the line that was to pass through Plea, the remains of an old stone barn had to be removed. When the workmen tore up the floorboards, they discovered, hidden in a hollow beneath the floor, wrapped in crumbling sheets of oilcloth, six stained glass windows.

When they were hauled up into the light and cleaned off, it was found that they were the representations of several saints, though what saints they might be was beyond the workmen's knowledge.

26

Over the course of the next several hours as stray visitors wandered into St. Bart's, either to pray or to escape the sudden heat, they were met with a mysterious sight. The lower portion of one of the stained glass windows on the east aisle was covered with a square of plywood. At the front of the church, standing in the sanctuary at the side of the altar, there was a vacuum cleaner. With its long cord snaking along the floor behind it like a leash, it looked like some mechanical pet that had wandered into the wrong yard. There was no sign anywhere of the caretaker, whose presence was normally as predictable as that of the statues perched upon their pedestals. A loose pile of church bulletins lay on one of the rear pews. Each time the door opened, a gust of wind blew along the aisle. The pile, as a result, was in disarray; several bulletins had blown off and lay scattered on the floor.

Scattered too were the pieces of glass on the table in the small room below. Mr. Berkeley sorted through them, but there was method in his movements now. He proceeded quickly, setting pieces one against another, turning them this way and that as one fits together the pieces of a jigsaw puzzle.

He worked as one in a trance, concentrating all his attention on the blank piece of cardboard on the table, as if the vision he so clearly saw there might disappear the moment his attention wandered. As he worked, his thoughts turned repeatedly to the experience he had had upstairs.

He had been close to finishing his dusting, when suddenly he had been startled by a sound – a high keening sound like a screech. At first he thought it was a car slamming on its brakes, but the sound grew steadily and swiftly in volume until it filled the echoing nave. He felt as if some unseen presence were bearing down upon him. He looked fitfully about, panicked, and felt his legs go liquid under him, as if he had been struck.

And then, just as suddenly as it had started, it stopped. And where the awful fear had been there was suddenly silence. He stood there utterly unnerved, the duster hanging slack in his hand, his heart hammering so loudly that it seemed to be beating against the ribbed vault of the church.

He glanced about and his gaze settled on the St. Francis window. He stared at it as if in a trance, and suddenly he realized he was seeing it whole. No sooner had the impossibility of that entered his thoughts than the vision vanished, and there in the lower panel stood the rough piece of plywood again.

But that brief vision of the window restored had been enough. He dropped everything he was doing and headed downstairs, threading his way along the winding passageway to his room.

And there he had worked steadily since, utterly unconscious of the passage of time, patiently sifting through the bits of colored glass, slowly piecing them back into the pattern he now held whole in his mind's eye.

27

As they bumped the buggy up the library steps, Charles watched the girl glance up at the gargoyle tooled in the stone above the entranceway – a fierce face peering out through a pattern of leaves. When he was small, Charles used to be afraid of the gargoyle. He would clutch his books to his beating heart and hurry by. The memory of that swept over him now as he came up the steps. The sound of the buggy bumping behind him melded with the memory of Emily bumping Albert's stroller up the stairs. For a moment he was more there than here.

The girl held the heavy wooden door open for him while he walked the buggy in. The sudden muting of the light, the instant hush, the coolness of the air against his sweaty skin – it was like entering a cave. The flyers tacked to the wall fluttered into silence as the door closed behind them. They crossed the narrow foyer, ascended a short flight of steps, and entered the rotunda, where the main desk stood. This had always been his favorite part of the library. The ceiling leapt two stories high and was crowned with a stained glass dome. Light broke through the dome and fell in colored fragments that seemed to float upon the marble floor. The floor itself was patterned in a series of concentric circles, as though the fall of light had set up some disturbance at the circle's center and sent the ripples riding outwards.

They waded into the room. To either side of the entranceway, a flight of stairs swept up to the second floor. There was a circular walkway with a marble railing that overlooked the well of the rotunda. He could remember standing up there as a small boy, peering down at the pattern of circles on the floor below. Opening off the rotunda to the left was the children's room; to the right, the adult section. Children were already gathering on the children's side for the Saturday Morning Club. Today it would be a puppet show. Through the entranceway, he could see that the puppet theater had been pulled out from the wall and set up in the alcove of the room.

The girl had wandered, meanwhile, to the center of the rotunda. She stood there bathed in colored light, with her head thrown back as she studied the design in the dome high overhead.

"It's roses," she said suddenly and, when she heard how the rotunda magnified her voice, a mischievous little smile crossed her face and she said it again, louder.

Almost instantly he heard a hurried tap of heels start along the hall that led to the staff room behind the main desk. He took the girl by the arm and ushered her quickly out of the rotunda and through the doorway into the adult section. The creak of the wrecked buggy wheel, which had risen to a shriek in the rotunda, dimmed instantly in the low-ceilinged, wood-paneled room. The tap of heels followed them as far as the entranceway, then stopped.

He headed straight for the alcove at the far side of the room. The alcove was the twin of the one on the children's side of the library. It was quiet and out of the way. There was a wooden table with no one sitting at it, and a window seat that followed the bulge of the large bay window that looked west onto a park. They sat down on the window seat with the buggy between them.

He glanced back at the doorway. A librarian stood there with a newspaper in her hand, her glasses hanging on a cord about her neck. She walked over and sat down at the desk just inside the doorway. She opened the paper and pretended to read while she peered over the top of it at them. She looked as if she was expecting trouble. She looked as if she was thinking that maybe they were planning on loading up the bundle buggy with books and selling them on street corners or something. She finally went back to her paper.

He sat with his elbows resting on his knees, while the sweat ran down his face and fell in lazy drops to the floor. There was a dull throb at the back of his head to go along with the one in his lip. He felt vaguely dizzy, as if he'd just been spun. As he stared down at the pattern of drops on the floor, he had the strange sense that the ground was not solid, that if he banged his foot down hard, the floor would shatter; and through the hole he had made he would see himself, lying curled in sleep, bits of broken shell scattered about the dreaming bed.

The alcove was cool and cast in shade. After a while the sweating stopped, and he began to feel a bit more human again. It was still pretty early on this side of the library. A couple of people sat at the long tables poring over newspapers attached to wooden poles, so that the open pages looked like the pinioned wings of strange wooden birds. Someone was busy feeding quarters to the photocopy machine. A woman with a better looking buggy than his was going through the paperback mysteries. That was about it.

The shelves in the alcove were set into the wall. The hand-lettered sign above the range closest to him read TRAVEL AND EXPLORATION. He ran his eyes over the spines of the books on the lower shelves. There didn't seem to be anything there about traveling the wilds of Caledon with a broken bundle buggy. He plucked something off the shelf at random and sat there with it open on his lap so that he'd have something to look busy with if the librarian happened to glance his way again.

It was a copy of *The Travels of Marco Polo*. He leafed through it a little as he sat there thinking of the mess he was in. A book in front of you was like some hole you were digging. Nobody bothered you while you were busy with it. You sort of dropped out of sight. Just the top of your head showing over the rim of the hole, the occasional shovelful of dirt thrown up. He dropped down into the hole now and glanced up over the edge of it every now and then at the librarian.

The girl sat beside him on the window seat, looking out into the park, running her finger through the dust on the deep ledge behind the window seat.

"I'm worried about the baby," she said.

"Don't be worried. I'm sure she has other dolls." They'd been through this several times now. Her mind went in small circles like a record stuck in a groove. She kept coming back to the baby.

"Maybe you have a younger brother or sister yourself," he suggested. "Maybe you come from a family with lots of kids."

"Yeah," she said, brightening at the idea. "Maybe I do."

But how had she gone from that to this? he wondered. He could compose any number of possible histories for her, but they all broke in pieces against the harsh reality of her homelessness.

The story he'd given to Gran on the phone had been at least half true; he had gone to the library. But the real reason for his going was in the hope that they might find something there that would somehow jog her memory. A book of names might be a good place to start. If she could just remember her name, the rest might follow.

He passed the time with Marco Polo while he worked up the nerve to approach the librarian. Marco had been barely seventeen when he set out from Venice with his father and uncle in the year 1271. Theirs was a perilous journey that would take them over uncharted seas, through hostile lands, and across the vast barren wastes of the Gobi Desert, before finally coming to the court of Kublai Khan. In light of all that, Charles figured he ought to be able to muster up the courage to cross the carpeted floor to the librarian's desk and ask to borrow a book of names.

The girl was still doodling in the dust.

"I'll be right back," he said to her. "You stay here and keep an eye on the buggy."

As he approached the desk, the librarian peered up over the rim of her paper at him. Her eye flitted over his face, paused at his smashed lip, dropped down and lingered over the picture of the train on his pajama top. He felt about five years old.

"Can I help you?" she asked, but she sounded like her heart wasn't really in it.

He made a quick change of plans.

"Can I have the key to the washroom?" he said.

She leaned and looked past him toward the alcove where the girl sat, then reached into the top drawer of the desk and came out with a key attached to a long wooden paddle. The word BOYS had been burned into the wood.

"Be sure to bring it back," she said, just in case he was thinking of taking off with the wood to build a house or something.

28

The boys' washroom was on the children's side of the library. He walked back across the rotunda and through the door on the opposite side. A sizable group had gathered for the puppet show. Today it was to be "Tattercoats."

The sight of the parents and children sitting there on the floor in front of the old puppet theater, waiting for the show to start, reminded him of all the times his sister Emily had trundled them off to the library for the Saturday Morning Club when they were small. Why had she done it? he wondered. To give mother a bit of a break, certainly. But there was more to it than that. It was like a duty she had laid upon herself – to wean them from the screen, to open other, inward worlds.

As he was standing there now, he spotted a set of encyclopedias on the wall by the door. He fanned through the first volume and found a brief entry on amnesia. He skimmed through it. It said that a state of amnesia could be brought on not only by a blow to the head, but also by drugs or alcoholism, or by some severe emotional shock. The memories in most cases were not really lost, but buried, and could ultimately be recovered. When the amnesia lasted for a long period, the patient was said to be in a fugue state, from the Latin *fuga*, meaning 'flight.'

He fumbled with the key in the washroom door. When he flicked on the light, he got his first good look at himself since the accident. It was not a pretty sight. His lip was all puffed up and purplish. The blood came from two cuts on top, probably made by his teeth. There was blood on his chin and spots of it spattered like sparks among the smoke from the steam engine on his pajama top. His face was streaked with sweat and smudged with ink where he'd wiped it with his hands, dirty from delivering the papers.

He washed himself clean with cool water, wet a wad of paper towel, dabbed gently at his lip, then tried to blot some of the blood from his pajama top. He wet his hair and finger-combed it, tucked the frayed ends of his cuff under, pinched the ends together where the shoulder seam was coming unstitched. If he'd had it to do all over again, he might have worn another top.

"This is a fine mess you've gotten yourself into," he said to his battered reflection in the mirror.

He thought he knew what he was doing when he got involved with this girl. She was in trouble. He was just trying to help her out a little. It was simple. He would take a quick dip into her life, then dash out again, like daring the frigid water of the lake on opening day. But it wasn't simple at all. He'd dipped in, all right, but he couldn't seem to dash out again. The thought of the phone call home reared its ugly head, right down to his hanging up on Gran in midsentence. There would be hell to pay for that. This couldn't just go on and on. He was going to have to start home soon.

He ran his fingers through his hair again as he looked in the mirror. The way his smashed lip twisted his mouth up on one side made him look a little like Elvis doing his famous sneer.

"Hi," he said to his reflection. "I was wondering if I could borrow a book of names."

"Excuse me?" The librarian slid the washroom key across the counter with the edge of her paper. It fell with a loud thud into the open drawer.

"A book of names," he repeated. The *m* sound came out kind of mangled.

"What kind of names?" she asked, suspiciously.

"First names," he said. "You know, like 'Charles,' 'Albert,' 'Elizabeth.' "

He was being as well mannered as he could manage under the circumstances. He imagined himself standing there in his blue blazer, with the fake handkerchief peeking from the breast pocket; his white shirt and tie, gray slacks, shoes freshly polished. He noticed her staring at the damp spots on his pajama top, where he had tried to blot the blood.

The librarian stole a look past him toward the alcove. The girl hadn't budged; neither had the buggy. The librarian put aside her paper and went over to the reference shelves. She ran her finger along a couple of rows, plucked out a book, and came back with it. She asked him for his library card. He said he didn't happen to have it with him; he explained that he didn't want to borrow the book, he just wanted to use it in the library. She said she needed the card for security, did he have any other ID? He said no, but he was just going to be sitting with it over there in the alcove. She thought about that for a minute, then handed him the book and told him to bring it back to her when he was finished with it. It seemed like everything in the building came back to her eventually.

The book was called *Name Your Baby*. It was an old paperback with a permabound cover. It looked like it had seen a lot of use. The corners of the pages were a little curled; some had been turned down to mark a place. The binding was cracked – a couple of the pages were loose and came out in his hand as he walked back to the alcove. He thought briefly about going back to the librarian and pointing out what kind of shape the book was in so that she wouldn't think he had done it, then thought better of it. He tucked the loose pages back in and kept on walking.

"Okay," he said to the girl as he sat down beside her on the window seat, "this is the plan. This is a book of names. I'm going to start reading out names and you tell me if one of them rings a bell."

"Okay," she said, but she didn't sound all that convinced it would work. He wasn't all that convinced himself, to tell the truth, but at least it was something.

The book was divided into two sections. The front half was devoted to girls' names, the back half to boys'. He started at the beginning of the *A's* with "Abigail," and just kept working his way through the list.

". . . Abra, Acacia, Acantha, Ada, Adah, Adalia, Adamina, Adar, Adda, Adela, Adelaide, Adeline, Adelle. . . ."

For the next half hour he sat there on the window seat, reading out names, while the girl looked out the window, doodled in the dust of the ledge, fiddled with the bent bars of the bundle buggy, or roamed restlessly around the alcove. Every now and then, someone would wander over in their direction, spot them there, and decide maybe they weren't that interested in travel and exploration after all.

". . . Cadence, Calandra, Calantha, Caledonia, Calida, Calista, Calla, Callula, Calvina, Calypso. . . ."

It was not exactly gripping reading. He'd never even heard of half of these names before. To break the monotony, he began skimming the notes beneath the names. The notes gave the root of the name, its meaning, variations on the name in other languages, nicknames, and a brief list of famous people with that name. He didn't bother reading all those bits aloud, or they would have been there well into next week.

It was obvious that parents-to-be had combed through the book, looking for names for the little bundle. Tick marks abounded in the margins. Pages had been turned down, possibilities circled in pencil. Each time he came across one of these things, he glanced instinctively over at the librarian, who was usually looking back, no doubt wondering what on earth they were doing there in the alcove reading aloud from the *Name Your Baby* book.

". . . Elizabeth, Ella, Ellen, Elma, Elmira, Elsa, Elva, Elvira, Elysia, Emerald, Emily –"

Someone had circled the name. He ran his eyes quickly through the entry: "Gothic: 'industrious one.' Nicknames: Em, Emmy. Famous people: Emily Brontë, English novelist; Emily Dickinson, American poet."

His sister Emily was a poet as well. He got a sudden clear image of her final incarnation before leaving home for college: her lithe body clad in black, loping down the street; the silences she spun about her; the shadows etched beneath her eyes; the air of one engaged in secret disciplines. She was a creature of the night; she courted darkness, stayed awake while others slept, composing poems in her cryptic scrawl on any scrap that came to hand.

She was like some exotic creature come among them, something from another century. The two of them remained close, but something had come into her that he could not share. He tiptoed to the edge of her and looked down on darkness. She, who had been his introduction to mystery, had herself become mystery.

The girl had turned from the window and was looking at him. "Who is Emily?" she said.

"I have a sister called Emily. Why?"

"I don't know. Nothing, I guess."

She went back to her doodling in the dust. At first he thought she had been merely playing around, but he took a closer look now and saw there was a pattern to it. The same group of signs, worked repeatedly. They looked like letters, but not English letters.

"Say, what is that you're doing there?"

"I don't know."

"It looks like some foreign language." He wondered again if she had come from some distant country, a stranger to Caledon. They stared together at the signs in the dust for a few minutes:

אמבריאל

They reminded him of something, though he couldn't put his finger on what it was. After a while he went back to reading the names. That went on for quite some time, until he felt himself falling into a sort of trance.

". . . Irma, Isa, Isabel, Isadora, Isis, Isolde –"

Suddenly the girl jumped up from the window seat and gave a little squeal. He almost had a heart attack.

"I remember," she said. "I remember." Loud enough that the librarian looked up from her paper. "I remember my name."

She grabbed his arm and started dancing him around the alcove. She was pretty excited, all right.

"Well, what is it?" he asked. "Tell me."

"Ambriel," she said. "It's Ambriel."

"Ambriel? You're sure?"

"Yes. Ambriel. It's Ambriel."

He wasn't sure he would have been quite so excited to find out his name was Ambriel, but at least it was a start.

For the library, however, it was a finish. The librarian practically flew across the floor to the alcove. She told them they'd have to leave.

"I'm Ambriel," said the girl.

The librarian said that was nice, but they'd still have to leave.

They quickly gathered up their things and creaked their way back out the door under her watchful eye. On the way down the steps, they ran into a couple of kids on their way to see the puppet show. Ambriel told *them* her name, too.

29

In the year 1295, after an absence of twenty-four years, Marco Polo returned to Venice with his father and uncle. According to legend, when the three of them, dressed in foreign clothes and haggard from the hard journey, knocked on the door of the family home, they were taken for beggars and turned away.

It was only after they had taken knives and slit open the seams of their robes, and streams of diamonds, emeralds, and rubies poured out, that they were finally recognized and welcomed home.

When you were walking a buggy, you noticed other people walking buggies. There was a kind of kinship between you. Charles would pass someone pulling a buggy and would give them a little nod, as if they both belonged to the same club. The trouble was, most people seemed as though they weren't too sure they wanted him in their club.

There were plenty of buggies around on a Saturday morning. Some were empty and folded flat, others had been pressed into service and carried their loads along as contentedly as packhorses. They did not have a wheel with a serious wobble; they did not rattle and shriek; they did not have a rotting egg box fused to their frame. They kept a wide berth as they whispered by on quiet wheels. Their owners didn't bother nodding back when he nodded at them. They were too busy looking at his buggy to notice him nodding.

About the only nod he got came from a guy pulling a buggy that could have been the long lost twin of his own. The guy was wearing a long woolen overcoat. He had a winter hat on, with the earflaps down. Where he was, it was another season entirely.

His buggy had a cardboard box fitted inside it too. It was crammed with dingy plastic bags, each bag filled to near bursting, their handles tied with bits of string. There were bags tied to the rim of the frame as well.

He moved along as slowly as the snail that bears its home on its back, scanning the ground as he walked. Suddenly he stopped. He bent down and snagged a butt tucked into the crack of the sidewalk. As he stood smoothing it out, he caught sight of Charles coming along with the buggy. Ambriel was walking a little ahead by herself, blazing their trail. Charles nodded and the guy's face lit up; he smiled across the seasons at him.

"Nice day, eh? Say, you want to watch that wheel, bud. Looks like she might come off on you."

"Thanks," said Charles, turning to take a look.

The guy noticed the neck of the guitar sticking out of the box. "See you got a guitar there. You play?"

"No, it's hers." Charles nodded in Ambriel's direction. She was standing at the corner up ahead, looking up and down the cross street, deciding which way to go.

"She your girl?"

"No, I'm just helping her."

"She sick?"

"No, she's lost."

The guy nodded, as if he knew what lost was like. He rounded the butt between his fingers, flicked a bit of dirt off the filter, then tucked it thoughtfully into the corner of his mouth. He started tapping his pockets, looking for a light.

The traffic light at the corner changed. Ambriel took a sudden turn and started across the street.

"I have to go," said Charles, taking off after her.

"You have a good day now," the guy called after him, still looking for a light. "And keep your eye on that wheel."

By the time Charles got to the corner, the light had changed again. He kept Ambriel in sight as she wandered off down the block by herself. That wasn't hard to do; apart from the guy with the plastic bags, she was about the only person on the street still wearing a coat. It could be they both lived in the same place.

He wondered how long it would take before she noticed he wasn't with her. He glanced up and down the cross street, but had no clear notion of where they were. The cool and quiet of the library had faded into memory now. He had hoped that remembering her name would lead to other revelations, but that hope had faded too with each block they walked in the wilting heat. She would amble along, then suddenly stop; and each time she stopped he was sure she had just had some momentous revelation, that some door had swung open in the darkness. It was this sense of imminence that urged him on.

He pinched his pajama top away from his sweaty skin, and wiped the perspiration from his forehead with his sleeve. A bakery nearby had its door propped open. The sweet smell of bread baking sent his thoughts to his stomach. It must be getting on toward noon. He'd spent the last of his money calling home. He wished now that he'd scooped up the toast Ambriel had left on her plate in the restaurant. He remembered the way she'd brought it to her mouth, paused, then put it back on her plate. There was something very strange about her. She worried him. He thought about the bag man asking him if she was his girl.

He took a look down the street. She had stopped midway down the block. She was standing there, looking down at something. He had a pretty good idea what it was. He'd seen this routine before. Several times now since they'd left the library, she'd stopped to pick up bits of glass, dropping them into the pocket of her coat. She was beginning to sound a little like a chandelier on legs.

He suddenly remembered the bag of food he'd brought from home. Had he left it in the church? No, he was sure he'd picked it up. He took a peek in the buggy. It was really starting to fill up. If they kept this up, he was going to have to hook a caboose onto the back of it. Along with the extra paper and the ball of wrappings and wire, there was now her guitar, his jacket, the rag doll the baby had dropped, one of the oranges from the bag her mother had spilled onto the sidewalk – but no sign of the bag of food.

He shifted the guitar, moved his jacket – and his heart sank. Lying there facedown, on top of the bag of food, was the *Name Your Baby* book from the library. He stared at it blankly for a moment, while the realization of what must have happened swept over him. In the hurry to pack things up, he had somehow packed away the book as well. The librarian would have noticed almost immediately that they'd made off with it. He wished it back onto the window seat in the alcove; he wished it back onto the shelf, where it had quietly sat with its loose pages and pencil-marked margins a secret to itself. But it stayed there facedown in the buggy, on top of the bag of food.

He picked up the book and saw a greasy stain on the side of the bag. The stain had transferred to the book. It had seeped into the page at the entry for "Rose" and sunk down as far as "Ophelia," six pages before. He quickly closed the book and tucked it under the newspaper at the bottom of the box.

The light changed from red to green, and he started across the street.

30

Color began as an accident in the making of glass. You set out to make white glass, and due to impurities in the sand or the ash, the glass came out colored. There were innumerable variables. Begin with beech wood ash and the white glass could turn saffron in the fire, and the saffron, if left longer, would turn reddish. Or the glass might turn from white to tawny, then deepen with time to a reddish purple.

If you liked the color, you ladled some out and set it aside. Take out some tawny to use for flesh color, heat the remainder for two hours longer and you got a reddish purple that could be used for robes. Some of the most magnificent colors were completely accidental. Unpredicted. Unrepeatable.

It was the French and the Germans who first mastered the art of making colored glass. Up until the sixteenth century, all the colored glass used in the English cathedral windows was imported from Germany and France. It was the French and the Germans who developed the technique of mixing metal oxides in with the sand and ash to create color in the glass. Add copper oxide for ruby glass, cobalt for blue, iron oxide for green, sulphur for yellow. But the oxides themselves often contained impurities, and the range of hues that resulted remained in large measure beyond the glassmaker's control.

It was the accidental beauty of the old glass that Mr. Berkeley loved. The quirks of color, the bubbles, the fogs, the bits of grit in the glass – flaws, you might call them, but flaws that let the light through in new ways, adding depth and shade to the design, waking the mystery in the work.

He felt the almost palpable presence of that mystery in the air now. He had handled many kinds of glass in his life, but not since those days in Canterbury had he held glass such as this. It pulsed with life. The feel of it in his hand was that of flesh to flesh.

There were any number of different ways in which the glass might have gone together. Still, when two pieces that had neighbored one another were brought together again, there was never any doubt of it. It was as if a charge passed between them, like a flash of lightning briefly illumining a darkened landscape. And a vivid image would flash into his mind with the force of a long forgotten memory coming once again to consciousness.

More than once while he worked, he had the sudden intuition that the table on which the pieces lay was, for a moment out of time, another table, the top of it as white as a fresh fall of snow, the pattern traced upon it like an intricate network of tracks. The walls of the room receded then, and in the corner he glimpsed a girl, achingly familiar, piecing the glass for a window at another table.

This sense of the room expanding was countered at other times by a sudden sense of contraction – a feeling of close confinement that swept over him unaccountably, so that he felt as if cocooned in cloth, coffined in the dark.

This, in its turn, would yield to the sudden feeling of being freed – the boards loosed, the bonds burst. The sense of being raised up, laid down in the light. The liquid play of light upon his limbs, the sense of its passing unimpeded through him, through all, so that for an instant the opaque stood translucent, and the scattered world was one.

31

They had probably issued an all points bulletin on the *Name Your Baby* book by now. Every time Charles saw a police cruiser coming down the street, he had to fight the urge to hunker down behind the nearest car until it went by. He slowed to a casual walk as a patrol car trawled past them now along the narrow street.

No doubt they looked odd, the two of them the only ones walking this sad stretch of street made up of auto body shops, engine rebuilders, auto repair places – all of them looking poorly. Mechanics poked their heads up from under the open hoods of cars as they passed. Pinschers, pit bulls, shepherds yowled as they strained against their chains, guarding their bit of ground.

Buildings petered out and fenced lots took their place. Mountains of discarded tires, bumpers stacked row on row on rusty racks, like ivory culled from the kill. Behind a high barbed fence, the shells of cars lay scattered over the barren ground. A huge crane swooped, caught one up in its claws, bore it effortlessly through the air, and dropped it into the yawning mouth of a compactor. There was a muffled crunch of metal, a soft *whoosh* as the windows exploded. Then the crane plucked the flattened mass from the slack jaws and added it to a sad pile, stacked like kindling for the fire.

Ambriel turned a bit of glass in her hand as she walked, running her thumb lightly around the edge of it. It was like she was following the faint trail of an elusive prey. She kept her eyes on the ground, scanning it purposefully, pausing now and then to study some piece of glass, as if it were a print, a dropping, some fragment of the fantastic coat of this strange beast they sought – Memory.

She would stop without warning, suddenly look around, cock her head to one side as though listening for some sound. He would listen along with her, yet hear nothing but the dim steady hum that was the city breathing. Was she straining to catch some faint cry laid over that? he wondered. Or feeling rather for some tear in the fabric, some sound that spilled from the inner side of it?

Or was she, after all, simply crazy? Cracked, shattered, broken long before the window fell on her? A little touched in the head, a bit buggy, as Gran would say? The thought nagged at him like a sliver in the skin. He picked and prodded at it, but only pushed it further in.

They walked on silently along the dead street. The sun beat down relentlessly; the rhythmic screaking of the buggy marked time. What would he do if the wheel did drop off?

he wondered. Would he take it as a sign? Would it signal his release, or would he simply feel called to shoulder the buggy and go on?

Their trek was taking them on a steadily southeasterly course through Caledon. But beyond knowing that, he was lost. They had ventured into an area unmapped in his mind. He tried to commit to memory the pattern of their turnings, but in this wasteland every street looked the same, and a vague unease reared its head as he looked back over his shoulder and realized he had lost the thread.

"Do you have any idea where we are?" he asked her.

"None at all," she said, looking around.

"That's what I figured."

"I feel like we're heading in the right direction, though."

"Great."

"What on earth am I doing here?" he muttered aloud as she stopped dead at yet another spill of glass, this one at the foot of a bombed-out factory wall. "I should have started back long ago. It must be after noon. Look at the state of me, all bashed up and bloody and sweating like a pig. Look at the state of Gran's buggy. She's going to kill me. I'm supposed to help her do the shopping. I'm supposed to take her to the hairdresser." He pictured Gran in her impatience with him, doing something she shouldn't: bending to make the beds, lifting the heavy laundry basket to take it down the stairs. And what if something was to happen to her? What then?

He was parched. He could barely work up the spit to speak. If he spotted a puddle, he would probably fling himself down in it face-first. Ambriel stooped and picked up a piece of the glass.

"Do you have to keep doing that?" he snapped.

"What?" she asked, turning the piece of glass in her hand.

"Picking up garbage like that."

"It's not garbage. It's glass."

"I know it's glass. But it's broken. It's lying on the ground. It's garbage."

She gave him a long, uncomprehending look.

"Forget it," he said. "Just forget it."

She began to turn the glass in her hand. It was sickle-shaped, like a sliver of moon dropped from the sky. Pale gray, pebbled in texture, almost opaque, yet suddenly translucent when she held it to the light.

He glanced up the blank face of the factory wall and saw a bank of windows two floors above. The dingy panes were a mishmash of various kinds and colors of glass. One of the panes in the bottom panel was broken. A piece of board covered the hole.

Ambriel was standing with her eyes closed now, the piece of glass clutched in her palm.

"Hey, be careful. You'll cut yourself," he said.

Her eyelids had begun to flicker a little.

"Ambriel, are you all right?" he said, but she didn't seem to hear him.

Then suddenly, "There was a fire," she said. "It was dark, and cold – so cold. There was fire – fire and ice."

He felt a shiver run through him.

She opened her eyes, like one waking from a dream. "We have to go that way," she said, pointing into the distance. She dropped the piece of glass into her pocket and started walking.

All thought of leaving her had instantly vanished. He grabbed the buggy and started after her. She was moving at quite a clip now. The buggy wheel was wobbling like crazy as he tried to keep up.

They walked for several blocks, then suddenly found their way barred by a high chain-link fence. They tried the next street over, and the one next to that, but they too were impassable. But as they turned down the third street, they found there was no fence. And where the others had dead-ended, they discovered a level crossing – two sets of tracks running side by side. He took a long look down them in either direction – and knew instantly where he was.

32

Coming from a railroad family, Charles found the pattern of the rail lines passing through Caledon etched upon his mind from an early age. He knew the sweep of the lines as they passed through the city, knew their origins and destinations, the names of the stops along the way, the points at which they merged with the main line, the points at which they branched off on their own. He knew the history of each as intimately as he knew the branchwork of veins on the back of his hand.

His family's history and that of the railroad were twinned in his mind. And at some point, if you looked far enough down the line, the two merged, and blood ran through the rails. Somewhere down there now, where the tracks veered north and took their course out of town, and the city lapsed into rolling hills and farmland, there was a tunnel – a tunnel not at all unlike the tunnel from which the steam engine on his pajama top was just emerging.

Sundays, when he was small, his father would often drive the children out to that spot, park the car on a patch of waste ground by an abandoned siding there, and wait for the Transcontinental to pass.

You would hear it first – a faint rumble of thunder in the dark of the tunnel – and then it would burst out into the light, like some sleek beast being born. As the silver cars flashed past, the children would sit on the hood of the car and wave, and the engineer would sound the horn.

He hadn't thought of those Sundays for a long time, but bumping the buggy over the tracks had somehow jarred the memory loose. And for an instant, a part of him here was also there, and something of the same awe that he had felt then as the train broke from the tunnel came over him now as he followed after Ambriel down the street. And the two moments were briefly one.

The wasteland through which they'd been walking was suddenly transformed on the far side of the tracks into a street lined with old trees and narrow row houses with brightly painted brick facades and postage stamp lawns.

On one of those lawns a sprinkler whirled about, sending plumes of water in intricate arcs over the grass. An old couple sat on the porch, surveying their estate. Their eyes widened a little as Ambriel loped by. She didn't so much as steal a glance at the sprinkler. Charles tried to follow her example, but as he drew even with the lawn and the fringe of spray swept across his shoes, his thirst got the better of him. He hopped the low fence, stopped the sprinkler in its whirling, and sucked back long draughts of the cool jet of spray. The couple looked speechlessly on.

When he could swallow no more, he set the sprinkler down and stepped back onto the sidewalk, soaked.

"Thanks," he said, as he grabbed the buggy and started after Ambriel. His wet shoes left vanishing prints on the pavement. The sun soon dried his clothes.

Ambriel led them through a labyrinth of streets. But now he had no need of the thread. They were back in his old neighborhood; he could have wound the way blindfolded.

Suddenly there were kids everywhere. The heat had lured them all outdoors. They were playing ball hockey on the road, skipping double Dutch on the sidewalk, congregating in noisy clusters on the porch stairs. Their conversations stopped abruptly as the two of them approached, heralded by the noisy creak of the buggy wheel. The skippers stilled their ropes and moved aside to let them pass. He could feel their quiet scrutiny, could hear the light titter of laughter rise up in their wake as the rhythmic slap of the ropes against the pavement resumed.

Caledon was rich in ravines. There was a time when you could walk from one end of town to the other, passing from one ravine system to the next, and only rarely have to rise up into civilization to cross a stray street before dropping back down to wilderness again.

Those days were long gone. The smaller ravines had been filled in. Where once there had been hollows, houses stood.

The larger ravines remained, scattered over the landscape, though the links between them had been broken. When he was young, his world had been bounded by those ravines. The dirt lane that ran behind their house dead-ended at the brink of one of them, and half his childhood had been spent scrambling down its steep sides and prowling the wilderness there.

The shop-lined street they were walking on now ran alongside a deep ravine. It followed them along like a wary companion, sometimes venturing quite near, at other times meandering off on its own. Now so close you could peer down from the street into the tangled depths of it; now just a faint glimpse of green between buildings.

He pretended not to know the place. He walked a little faster, trying to keep his breathing even, trying to quell the emotion that wanted to spring up inside. It was a little like walking past a large dog off its leash; if you kept your eyes averted and your pace unwavering, perhaps it would pay you no mind.

The ravine had fallen on evil days since he'd last been here. They passed a block of buildings bordering it – vacant all, their doorways boarded shut, plywood where windows once had been. Beside them, an empty lot with a realtor's sign staked in the soil. The waste ground was littered with garbage. Nobody belonged to it; nobody cared for it; nobody picked up the trash that made its way there. You had the sense that some large beast was poised to spring and swallow all memory of the place forever.

He glanced across the lot, across the canopy of trees that showed above the gap of the ravine. His gaze settled momentarily on the field on the far side, then flitted away. He bumped the buggy down the curb at the corner, crossed the street, and had bumped it up the opposite curb before he realized Ambriel was no longer with him.

She had turned down the street. He saw her standing on the low concrete bridge that spanned the ravine. He watched as she leaned over the railing and peered down into the ravine for a moment, then straightened and walked on.

A little farther along the street there was a level crossing. A set of signal lights and a worn wooden sign in the shape of an *X* marked the spot. But she didn't walk as far as the tracks. On the far side of the bridge she took a sudden right turn, leaving the sidewalk behind, wading into the weeds and scrub grass that bordered the ravine. She moved slowly, but with that strange sense of purpose she had about her. Fifty yards into the field she stopped.

Charles felt as if he'd been punched in the stomach. He stood rooted to the spot for a long time, watching. Finally, he turned and followed her. He crossed the bridge and pulled the buggy through the weeds and wild grass – the brittle brown stalks of last year's growth woven in with the new green. He had hoped to be able to slip quietly past this place. Yet by some uncanny intuition, she had been led to the precise spot.

33

"What's up?" he asked, as calmly as he could manage.

"I don't know. Something." She stared dead ahead, her senses tuned to some unseen stimulus.

Charles looked about. There was no one else in sight, and yet the place felt full of people. You could almost see the impress of ghost feet in the long grass, feel a slight thickening of the air where they stood.

At first sight it was an ordinary spot of ground, indistinguishable from any other section in the long swath of right-of-way that flanked the rail lines as they cut through Caledon. Scrub ground, tenanted only by the high towers that held the power lines aloft.

But as you stood awhile on the spot, your eye fell on, here, a piece of roof tile lying in the long grass; there, a blackened brick; there, a bit of broken molding tucked among the weeds. And then, the eye alerted, you noticed other oddities: a rosebush in the midst of the wild grass; an old lilac, the air already laced with the disturbing scent of its blooms; a set of concrete steps, not simply dumped there, but rooted to the spot where they stood, leading nowhere.

Soon you began to discern the faint outline of the cellar hole of the building that had once stood here, the walls razed to ground level, the hole filled in and covered now with the same ragged blanket of grass and weed that grew over all.

They stood there awhile side by side. Then Ambriel walked over to where the rosebush grew by the steps, bent down, and plucked from the ground a shard of glass. She brushed away the dirt and revealed a frostlike pattern etched lightly in the surface of it.

Charles took one look at it – and up from the weeds and rubble there rose a winter night of fire and ice, whole and entire before his mind's eye.

He had been jarred awake just past midnight that night by the ringing of the phone. His father had answered it. He lay half awake listening to the sleep-thickened voice, heard the sudden note of alarm that entered that voice, felt the long silence that followed. Mother must have heard it as well, for by the time Father had hung up the phone, she was in the kitchen with him.

"What is it?" she asked.

"The depot's on fire," he said. "I have to go down there."

While his father dressed, Charles scrambled out of bed and pulled on his own clothes in the dark of the room. By the time his father appeared in the hall for his coat, Charles was fully dressed and waiting by the door. He pleaded with his father to take him, and finally he relented.

It was bitterly cold. Earlier in the day it had snowed, but now the sky was clear and strewn with stars. A sliver of moon sailed the treetops as the car crept along the sleeping streets. His father said nothing.

The depot was the old Caledon railway station, a historic building well over a hundred years old. Several years back, the building, abandoned and fallen into a sad state of disrepair, had been slated for demolition by the railroad. It was his father, in league with the Caledon Historical Society, who had saved the depot by proposing to city council that it be renovated and turned into a railway museum. Council had agreed to the proposal and, for the past several years, Father had spent a good deal of his spare time overseeing the operation of the new museum. It was a labor of love.

They saw the thick cloud of smoke billowing into the air long before they arrived at the site. There were four fire trucks already on the scene, their hoses crisscrossing the roadway like a nest of enormous snakes in the moonlight. The police had set flares in the middle of the road and had blocked off all traffic through the area. They parked the car as close as they could and walked to the site.

He had never seen such a fire. The whole roof of the depot was a moving mass of flames. Perched high atop a ladder rising from one of the trucks, a firefighter directed a plume of water down on the blaze. Floodlights mounted on the trucks lit the area around the building.

It was a strange and unsettling marriage of opposites: the bitter cold of the night and the heat of the fire; the brightness of flame and floodlight in the midst of thick darkness; the great plume of smoke ascending into the cloudless sky.

The backlit figures of the firefighters were like shadow puppets, acting out some silent drama on a stage. The first crew on the scene had managed to rescue some of the valuables from the building. A dozen display cases sat out in the snowbound field like some bizarre exhibition set up out-of-doors. Father moved among them, peering down through the smoky glass, identifying the survivors – the calm of the cases sitting out in the snow in contrast with the confusion of the fire.

Curious neighbors had emerged from houses along the nearby streets. With their coats thrown over their night-clothes and their eyes heavy with sleep, they stood around in quiet clusters, watching.

The entire scene had about it the quality of a dream for Charles as he stood in the snowy field with his father, feeling numbed with cold, with fatigue, with the shock of seeing this place so much a part of their lives fallen to the mercy of the fire. From time to time he would glance up into his father's eyes and see the flames reflected there.

Now and then the shrill wail of a siren would cut the night and yet another fire truck would arrive on the scene. They smashed the windows with their axes and trained their hoses on them, but the fury of the blaze forced them back.

It was clear the building was beyond saving. Finally, with a muted roar, the roof collapsed into the interior, and Charles crawled off to the car and fell asleep.

By dawn, when the hoses had all been reeled in and the trucks had gone, all that remained in their wake was the shell of the building, still smoldering, sheathed entirely in ice. As it stood shimmering in the early light, it was as though the depot had been whisked away in the night and some fairy palace composed of crystal set in its place.

Later that day he had come back with his father and a couple of the members of the historical society to retrieve the display cases from the field. The ice had melted in the sun. In the clear light of day, the building was no longer a fairy palace, but a sad ruin. It sat there broken, its windows shattered, the wood charred and blistered, the brick blackened by the blaze.

He walked silently by his father's side around the sodden remains. The roof was gone, stumps of charred wood jutted from the wall where the ceiling beams had been. The interior was completely gutted. The floor had been consumed by the blaze. There was a clear view through to the cellar, choked with ash and cinders that had once been roof and floor and ceiling. The only things still in place inside were a safe bolted to the brick wall, suspended over emptiness now; the exposed network of heating pipes branching through the empty space; the random bloom of a radiator coiled against a wall; the chimney stack rising unscathed from the midst of the ruins. Nothing more.

They loaded the smoke-damaged display cases into the back of a pickup truck and drove away.

Something had shattered inside his father the night of that fire. Some bright shard had fallen into the snowy field and been lost forever.

The memory faded, and Charles found himself standing in the empty field this May morning with Ambriel.

"There was a fire here," she said. "It happened at night. In the winter. I remember fire. I remember ice."

"Yes," he said, "there was a fire. Four years ago the old train depot that stood here burned down. I was here." He stood looking at her a moment, filled with amazement. "You must have been here, too," he said. "Don't you see what that means, Ambriel? It means you must live in Caledon. It means you probably live nearby. How else could you have been here in the middle of the night that night?"

The thought that one of the slippered figures standing about in the cold that night was her was strange, and stranger still the two of them standing here again now, their lives linked suddenly by memory.

Without memory, what was there here? Only the wasteland, the scrub grass and weeds, the riddle of the lilac and the rosebush, the hints and guesses hidden in the grass: the charred bricks, the broken molding, the steps leading nowhere. Only the empty field and the sudden drop into the dark of the ravine.

They walked back to the sidewalk. He stopped to untangle a rubbery stem of bindweed that had wrapped itself around the axle of the wheel.

He glanced past the level crossing and down the street, lined on either side with houses. There they stood, stone-faced and still. Yet each one held its history, told its own tale of joy and sorrow. If they were to start down this street now, knocking on every door, how long would it take until they came to that door whose opening would open all?

34

Charles looked at his watch. It was twelve o'clock. It was always twelve o'clock. He tapped the face of it twice, hard, with the tip of his finger – to no effect. He shook his arm vigorously and checked again, but the sweep hand stood as still as stone.

"Well?" he asked. Ambriel was standing beside him, looking intently at a house across the street. It was a bungalow. For some reason she was drawn to bungalows. There were a lot of bungalows in this neighborhood. They had stopped in front of a lot of houses.

"No," she said, and started walking again.

It had been his suggestion that they investigate the streets in the immediate vicinity of the depot site, on the theory that if she had witnessed the fire there was a good chance she lived in the neighborhood.

They had threaded their way up and down a dozen streets bordering the site, stopping while she scrutinized a house, starting up again. Stopping, starting again. The first few times she had stopped, he was sure she had found her house, but by the time the same scenario had repeated itself for the umpteenth time, his enthusiasm had begun to wane. He was worried as well that someone watching from one of the houses would find their actions odd, and take it into their heads to call the police. That was the last thing he wanted, so when she turned and took a sudden course southward, away from the site, he abandoned the island of shade he'd been standing in and followed after her without complaint.

They passed through neighborhoods he knew, through neighborhoods he had never seen before, through posh neighborhoods and poor neighborhoods, through old neighborhoods and new neighborhoods. And it came clear to him that Caledon was not one thing only, but an intricate pattern of pieces come together.

Now and again, as they walked, the madness of what he was doing would sweep over him. His heart would start to race, his breath come short and sharp, and a sudden panic would rise up inside him. Yet each time it came he would push the panic down again and go on.

He had always been the timid one: quiet, pliant, eager to please. It was that quiet that had kept him somehow on course through the dark time, when their lives had been shattered with a soft *whoosh*, like the windows of the car in the compactor. It was he who had been the calm one in the midst of the chaos of the move; he who had prowled the streets, pulling the wagon behind him, hunting down the endless boxes to pack away the pieces of their lives.

But had he ever done one totally mad thing in his life before today? There was skipping the piano lessons, of course, but somehow that was part of this. He cast his mind back. Once, years ago, on a dare from Elizabeth, he had walked out along the narrow wooden plank that ran below the billboard anchored at the edge of the ravine. He had walked all the way out to the end, paused long enough to look down into the green dark, then made his way quickly back along the yielding plank on legs gone liquid with fear. But that had been different, something over and done with in a minute. And there was no one daring him down this plank that stretched on endlessly into day.

There was nothing really, nothing but this fear he felt that if he was to leave this girl, he would leave with her some vital piece of himself; that if he was to break faith with her now, brokenness would be his fate. And so he kept on, hoping against hope that some revelation might lie just around the next corner, that the key might somehow lie couched in the next bit of glass she plucked from the street.

The sidewalk was pooled with shadow beneath the trees. The maples were shedding their gold-green flowers in the sudden heat. Drifts of them blanketed the shadows and clung to the buggy's wheels as they waded through.

Old pavement, new pavement – the repeating pattern of squares. The record of when each section had been laid stamped in the concrete. The rhythmic bump of the buggy over the cracks, the grating of the wheel against the frame – the steady pulse of the two throbbing through the frame to his hand. The strange feeling that the buggy branched from his fingers, flesh of his flesh, that the blood pumping through his veins pumped as well through the battered tubing of it.

Here a game of hopscotch chalked on the sidewalk, there a rainbow. Records of passing that the next rain would wash away. Other passings were more permanent. Bottle caps and bits of glass embedded in the asphalt of the road, like fossils in rock. Footprints, paw prints, the dim imprint of names scratched in the once wet concrete.

And suddenly, among these random markings, a memory. He stumbled on it unexpectedly, as Ambriel stumbled on her bits of glass. He picked it up, turned it in his hand, ran the thumb of his thoughts over the sharp edge of it – and saw a summer's day when he was seven.

He had been awakened that morning by the sound of jackhammers outside the house. He went to the front window and saw a work crew taking up the stretch of sidewalk that ran in front of their house.

He stationed himself at the living room window for the better part of the day, oblivious to the enticements of the tube behind him, to the sounds of battle that broke out from time to time between Elizabeth and Albert the Terrible. Emily, who was on duty that day, had brought him his lunch and stayed to watch with him awhile.

First, the crew had drilled into the old concrete, breaking it into large pieces, then breaking those pieces down to smaller pieces with a sledgehammer. They loaded those onto the back of a truck and drove off.

A little later a second crew came and built a wooden form around the edges of the hole the first had left. As they were finishing, a cement truck appeared. Fresh concrete flowed down the chute as the truck inched along and slowly filled the form. The workers spread the concrete evenly to the edges with a rake, smoothed it with wooden floats, laid the seams in place; they etched the concrete, stamped it, drew the bristles of a new broom lightly over the surface of it. Finally, they set up wooden trestles to warn people away from the wet concrete, and drove away.

By that time all four of them were stationed at the window, waiting. Swearing them all to secrecy, Emily had hatched a plan. One by one they went down to the edge of the wet concrete farthest from the house and set the prints of their hands in the pavement, side by side. It would be a record of them for the future, she said – there for years and years.

Near dark, a solitary workman came back and removed the barriers. He saw the prints, but the concrete was already dry.

Almost every day after that, they walked across that patch of concrete in their comings and goings. Time passed, and they all grew older, but the memory of them that summer day remained fixed in the pattern of handprints in the pavement. And when it rained, the water lingered in the marks they'd made.

He hadn't thought of that in ages, but now he seemed to come upon pieces of memory at every turn. It was being with Ambriel that was the reason behind it. The more she searched, the more he seemed to find. He dropped this piece in his pocket, where it rattled about with all the other bits he had picked up that day.

Is that what memory was? Stray bits dropped in a pocket, making their muted music as you moved along? Was there some sense to them, some pattern to the pieces? Did they tell a story, like the stories in the stained glass at St. Bart's?

There was an outside and an inside to things. There was him walking here on this spring day through the streets of Caledon. And at the same time, there was him moving inwardly from thought to thought, from memory to memory. Sometimes walking, yes – but sometimes flying; sometimes groping blindly through the mazy dark; sometimes gliding like a boat on a stream; sometimes inching uncertainly up a sheer wall of stone.

There were maps of Caledon. On the wall at home there was that early map – the lots laid out in blocks and lozenges, the regular pattern of roads and rail lines already clear. But what maps were there for this inward moving?

35

From time to time as he worked, Mr. Berkeley turned to look behind him, half expecting to find someone standing there in the room with him. This sense of presence grew stronger as time passed and the glass came slowly together. While he worked he found his gaze returned repeatedly to the face he had set at the center of the pattern. It was so very real, the face of someone he seemed to know, someone he had somehow known all his life.

He had begun to repiece the window first from the corners. One corner had remained more or less intact and provided the pattern for the others. He grouped the glass by color, by shape, by size, taking up a likely bit and turning it this way and that, like a child at a puzzle, until the piece found its home.

With the four corners in place, he turned his attention next to the medallion at the center in which the figure stood. An oak-leaf border ran about the rim of the medallion. He ferreted out all the pieces on which traces of that pattern were painted, and began slowly to piece the circle.

Those strange impressions he had experienced earlier continued to flash with stunning intensity into his mind while he worked – as though they were somehow stored in the glass, suspended there along with the bubbles and the bits of grit.

And woven in with them now, images of a different sort. Fragments, it seemed, from the stories of the desert saints. The feeling of heat, of thirst, the weariness of endless walking. And threading through all, the rhythmic creaking of a turning wheel.

36

"The swelling has started to go down," she said, leaning over to look at his lip as they walked along. He ran the tip of his tongue over it. There was a salty taste from the blood that had dried on the cut.

The street sloped gently away, and in the distance you could see the lake, like a sliver of glass shimmering in the sunlight. When the wind came up off the water now, there was a coolness to it. They had entered the artists' quarter of Caledon, one of the oldest parts of the city. Many of the buildings that lined the street dated back well over a hundred years. When you looked up along the rooflines, you caught a glimpse of the city as it was then; when you looked down, it was now.

The street was a busy nest of narrow, brightly painted shops. There were several small galleries, with paintings and pieces of sculpture displayed in their windows; funky clothing stores; small smoky clubs; bookshops with bins ranged on the street; cafés on every corner. With the warm weather, the cafés had spilled out onto the street. Couples sat at small round tables, sipping coffee, basking in the sun like turtles on a rock, while the motley crowd flowed past.

For the first time that day, he did not feel as if all eyes were fixed on them. In so varied a blend they barely warranted a glance. The music piping out onto the street from the shops drowned out the creaking of the buggy wheel; his pajama top, with the picture of the train on it, could have been culled from a bin at the back of any number of the shops on the street; Ambriel, shuffling along in her black boots and her long coat, with her spiked hair and her lean looks, could have been some young artist lured out onto the street from her dim garret by the warm sun.

Perhaps she lived here? Perhaps she was, in fact, an artist? A musician perhaps, busking on corners to get by, living with friends in a room around here.

He was beginning to think she'd been a little strange long before the window fell on her. At one point while they were walking, she turned to him and said, "It's as if I've fallen out of myself. Once I find the way back in again, I'll be home." He was no closer to understanding her strangeness, but he'd begun to learn his way around in it a little.

She walked idly along, pausing every now and then to peer into the window of a shop. He looked for a glimmer of recognition in the eyes of the people who passed by her. But there was nothing.

They were nearing a corner when she stopped suddenly and looked up at the sign that hung out onto the street in front of a secondhand bookstore. It was a painted wooden sign, suspended from a rusty pole by two metal hooks. The wind off the lake had lifted a little, and the sign swung in the breeze, making a gentle creaking sound that answered that of the buggy wheel.

It was an odd sign, much older than any of the others along the street. The paint was weathered; a web of fine cracks ran through the wood. He thought about how long it must have hung there, creaking lightly in the wind, while time transformed the street around it.

The wood had been carved with exceptional skill. The design was dominated by a figure – the face of a man that appeared to have pushed itself out from the flat plane of the wood and so entered the world.

The figure was painted a deep green. Its long hair and beard had been meticulously carved to resemble foliage, and from either corner of its open mouth there issued the thick stalk of a vine. The vines curled upward and wound their leafy length along the edge of the sign until they met below in the middle, where they branched into the ornamented letters that spelled the name of the shop: THE GREEN MAN.

There was something about the intricately carved foliage that reminded him of the stonework that crowned the pillars in St. Bart's. There was something in the figure itself that reminded him of the face tooled in the stone above the library door. But that had been a fearful face. This, for all its strangeness, did not so much strike a chord of fear as one of mystery. It was almost as if the figure were laughing – and its laughter was the leaves; or speaking – and its words were the winding vines.

Ambriel had walked over and was peering in the window of the shop. There were a couple of bins of weathered books out on the street in front of the shop, but the place itself appeared empty. A sign hung in the door: the words BE BACK AT above a clockface with movable hands. The hands were positioned at twelve o'clock.

"There's something familiar about this place," said Ambriel. "I feel as if I've been here before." She cupped her hands to the glass and looked in. He stood beside her and did the same.

It was a long, narrow shop. The walls were lined with tall wooden bookcases. In the gaps between the cases, clusters of pictures were hung upon the wall. Two long rows of lower bookcases were ranged along the floor the length of the shop, making three narrow aisles. At the back of the shop, Charles could see a desk stacked with books. There was a lamp on it, and for a moment he imagined he saw a thin stream of smoke rising in the still air.

As always when she stopped like this, he was sure some revelation was at hand. The sign creaked lightly in the wind; the fringe of the slack awning, in whose shade they now stood, flapped in the breeze like a lazy beating of wings. He watched as she ran her eyes over the books in the window. They were an eclectic mix, ranged seemingly at random over an expanse of dusty green velvet. There were novels new and old, coffee table books, biographies, cookbooks, travel books – each of them flagged with a slip of paper bearing the price.

His eye skimmed lightly over them – and suddenly stopped. For tucked among the books at the back of the display, half-hidden by a history of Caledon, was a copy of *A Wonder Book of Tales for Boys and Girls*. He thought at first he must be imagining it. He turned to glance at Ambriel, and saw that her gaze had settled on it as well.

Unlike the copy at home, this one was in mint condition. The cloth was not faded, the binding was not frayed. Under the price on the flag of paper that protruded from the book, the shop owner had written the word RARE.

He stood there in the patch of shade under the awning, and it was as if the noise of the street was suddenly stilled. And up from the pages of the book, as clear to his ear as if she stood beside him now, came the sound of Emily's voice, reading from the *Wonder Book*.

It was not the shadow of a memory, not the dried flower pressed between the pages, the color faded, the perfume fled – not that; but the bloom full on the bough, the thing itself. So that, as he stood now staring at his ghostly reflection in the window of the shop, his inward self could feel the soft press of the bedsprings against him as he lay across Emily's bed and listened to her read. His inward self could press his nose to the quilt that covered the bed and smell it still, could run his finger over the several fabrics that formed the patches, feel those that had worn sooner than others, study the repeating pattern of the pieces.

Of all the books she had read to him back then on his Saturday morning visits to her room, the *Wonder Book* had been his favorite. It was the one most steeped in magic – and it was magic he had craved then more than anything in the world. The adventures of King Arthur and the

Knights of the Round Table, the voyages of Sinbad, the wanderings of Odysseus, the enchanted forest of fairy tales, steeped in fear and wonder.

As she read, the scene would rise in his mind, the figures in the stories take flesh, worlds arise before his inward eye. Lying listening to her, he was Ali Baba hidden among the leaves of the tree, while she mouthed the magic words that opened the door in the wall of stone and revealed the treasure within.

He devoured those stories, and they became part of him. When they finished reading, he would leave the house and find himself suddenly in a world transformed. He would wander along the dirt lane behind the house and drop down into the ravine, where he would play out the adventures he had heard. The world was no longer one unyielding thing, but many things at once, each overlaying the other. The lane was no longer simply this lane, the ravine no longer simply itself. He had the overwhelming sense that behind the show of the things, some great mystery lay couched.

Standing now in this bit of shade beside this strange girl, he had that same sense again – the sense that the world was a far more mysterious place than he normally found it to be. The sense that at the beating heart of this quite ordinary place something extraordinary stirred.

His reverie was broken by a movement in the depths of the shop. A figure emerged from the shadows there and walked toward the desk. As the figure moved into the lamplight, he saw that it was an old woman carrying an armload of books. She set the books down on the desk, plucked the end of a cigarette from the ashtray, took one final drag, then butted it out. She leaned down as she did so and, glancing toward the front of the shop, saw him standing at the window. Their eyes met – and for one long, impossible moment he could have sworn he was looking into Emily's eyes, peering from this old woman's face.

The woman reached for the glasses that hung on a cord about her neck, put them on, and looked at him again. She came around the desk and began walking slowly toward the front of the shop.

Charles turned and found himself standing at the window alone. Ambriel had vanished.

37

He grabbed the buggy and started off down the street, searching for her. She was nowhere in sight. As the minutes passed and he failed to find her, a small voice inside him whispered that now was his chance to turn around and head back home. He listened, but he kept looking all the same, hoping against hope that he hadn't lost her.

He stopped at the first corner he came to and glanced down the side street. It was a short block of sedate old houses with a high fieldstone wall at one end. Halfway down the block, heading straight toward it, he spotted a familiar figure loping casually along.

The warm sun had enticed the inhabitants from their houses. Someone was perched on a ladder, washing windows. A willowy old woman was rooting dead leaves out from around her rosebushes with a rake. A guy in shorts and a muscle shirt was washing his car at curbside with a hose.

It was a quiet street. The people who lived there knew who belonged on it. Strangers stuck out. Strangers with squealing bundle buggies stuck out more. He could feel all eyes on him as he hurried after Ambriel down the street.

A river of soapy water ran along the curb and dropped through a sewer grating near the base of the wall. A boy of about five had parked his tricycle at the edge of the sidewalk. He had collected a pile of twigs and was squatting down by the curb, dropping them one by one into the water, watching them sail down the short stretch of street and disappear through the sewer grating.

Ambriel had stopped to watch, but the boy was so absorbed in what he was doing that he hadn't noticed her. The sound of the buggy broke upon his play. He glanced up and took in the strangers with a quick glance. Ambriel smiled at him.

"Hello," she said. "What are you doing?"

"Playing boats. Who are you?"

"Ambriel," she said, as if it were a tricky question she just happened to know the answer to.

The boy looked at Charles. "What happened to your mouth?" he asked.

"I fell."

"Me, too," said the boy, and he pulled up his pant leg to show a bandaged shin. "You should tell your mommy to give *you* a bandage," he said solemnly.

"I will when I get home," he said. If he ever got home.

"Why are you wearing those funny clothes?" asked the boy.

Charles looked down at his pajama top. He thought briefly about putting his jacket back on, but it was far too hot. The boy was looking past him now at the buggy. He had noticed the neck of the guitar sticking out of it.

"What's that you got there?"

"A guitar."

"Can you play it?"

"No, it belongs to her." He gestured behind him to where Ambriel had been standing. The boy looked, then looked up. His mouth fell open.

Charles turned and found Ambriel sitting calmly atop the wall.

"Hello, down there," she said.

"How on earth did you get up there?" he asked.

"Easy. You should see the other side. It's beautiful. Here, pass the buggy up."

"You're not serious."

"Perfectly serious. Come on, pass it up."

Charles turned to the little boy and gave a helpless shrug. He wheeled the buggy over to the base of the wall. Grabbing it from the bottom, he lifted it up over his head. Ambriel leaned down, took it by the handle, and hoisted it up to the top of the wall beside her. Gripping the edge of the wall with one hand, she began to lower it slowly down the other side.

"Be careful with that," he said – just as she let go of the buggy. A muffled crash came from the far side of the wall as it hit bottom. The guitar let out a little *twang* that hung for an instant in the air.

"That was maybe not such a good idea," he said.

"Don't worry. It's fine. Okay, your turn now." She leaned down and held out her hand to him.

Charles glanced back at the little boy, who was still standing there openmouthed. For him this wall marked the rim of the known world. He had never seen anyone go over it before. Something between fear and awe was etched in his eyes.

Charles reached up and Ambriel gripped him around the wrist. As he scrambled for footholds on the smooth fieldstone, she hauled him up. Suddenly, there they were, the two of them sitting astride the wall. She was exultant. He'd never seen her quite so happy.

The ground looked a long way down. On the one side, the sun-drenched street and the little boy looking up at them; on the other, a sudden wilderness, a band of woods that followed the bend of the wall away into the distance. It was shocking to see the two worlds set side by side, the one oblivious to the other, with only the breadth of the wall between them.

The rich smell of soil and leaf mold wafted up from the wilderness side. In the mottled shade at the base of the wall, he could see the buggy lying on its side. The stuff inside had spilled out onto the ground beside it.

Ambriel waved good-bye to the little boy and lowered herself down the far side of the wall, letting herself drop the last couple of feet to the ground.

Charles took one last look down the street. The memory of all the many streets they had wandered down that day swept over him. He followed the maze of them in his mind, all the way to this last turning.

The sun stood high in the sky. From his perch he could see what must have been the back of The Green Man. It appeared that someone lived above the shop, for as he was watching, a door opened and a girl came out onto a deck, carrying a large box. She glanced his way and saw him sitting there on the wall. A strange expression came over her face. She set the box down and stood looking at him.

He could hear the sound of the water spilling through the sewer grating. The little boy was staring up at him with a worried look on his face.

"Don't worry," said Charles. "Everything's going to be all right." Then he took hold of the top of the wall and swung himself down the far side.

IV

The Girl in the Glass

Quick now, here, now, always –

T. S. Eliot, *Four Quartets*

38

In 1852, when Joseph Connolly donated a parcel of his land on the northern outskirts of Caledon for the building of a new church, it was decided that the church should be built after the manner of the great Gothic churches of England. After centuries of neglect, the Gothic or "pointed" style had seen a recent revival.

One of the champions of the new style was the young architect Lawrence Linton, who had recently immigrated to Canada from England and set up shop in Caledon. Linton was awarded the commission for the building of St. Bartholomew's, as the new church was to be called. It marked the beginning of a long and illustrious career that was to set its mark upon the face of Caledon. But that is another story.

The site for the new church was located on the crest of a wooded hill. Linton oversaw every aspect of the construction, from the laying of the foundations to the design of the furnishings. Most of the materials used were of local manufacture, though the black quartz and marble required for the pillars and capitals of the interior had to be imported from abroad. They were brought by ship to harbor, then hauled by horse and cart through the mire of muddy roads to the building site.

Slowly the structure rose from the surrounding woods. The outer walls, hung with scaffolding, appeared from a distance like some fantastic web spun over the stone. Once the walls were raised, the open timber roof was set in place like a lid on a jewel box.

Meanwhile, stonemasons began their skilled work on the interior. Sculpted figures ornamented the porch about the main doors. The capitals that crowned the columns of the nave were dressed with delicate patterns of leaves carved from the stone. In high and hidden places their imaginations brought forth whimsical creatures. Here, a pair of small pigs tucked under a stone leaf. There, a stone cat curled atop a capital, quietly watching a wary mouse. There, a small caterpillar inching its way along a carved leaf. It was as though the church had been dipped whole into a teeming pool and risen dripping with all manner of life.

Finally, the windows were installed. They were initially of clear glass patterned with paints to give the effect of grisaille windows. As time passed and money came forward from donors, these first windows were gradually replaced with stained glass. Often a window would be dedicated by a wealthy patron to the memory of a family member who had died.

As a result, the windows of St. Bart's were in a range of styles and were the work of many manufacturers. Stained glass was not produced locally in Caledon until the end of the nineteenth century. The first windows came from England and France, ordered from catalogs and produced by the large stained glass houses that flourished then in those countries. These windows were rarely signed, and so, with the passing of years, their history grew uncertain.

Among the earliest of the stained glass installations in St. Bart's was a set of two windows of obscure origin acquired by the architect Linton himself and dedicated to the memory of his wife, who had died in childbed.

39

The fall from the wall hadn't done the buggy much good. It lay on its side by a bush at the base of the wall, one wheel in the air. Charles righted it and reloaded the stuff that had spilled out onto the spongy ground. Another handful of pages had fluttered loose from the *Name Your Baby* book. He tapped them back into place and buried the book at the bottom of the buggy. The front page of the leftover paper was crumpled. He smoothed it out as well as he could, brushed the bits of leaf mold from the doll's dress and his jacket, rooted out the orange from under the bush where it had rolled, pressed the foil pack of date squares back into shape, and settled everything back inside the buggy as carefully as if he were packing up his suitcase for the cottage.

Ambriel inspected the guitar, gave it a light strum, then slung it over her shoulder. They started walking. After hours of tramping the hot pavement, he luxuriated in the soft yield of the leaf mold underfoot, the coolness of the woods against his skin, the damp rich smell of the soil-scented air.

A hush lay over all – the same hush he had sometimes felt at St. Bart's. As he looked along the narrow path, it was as if he were walking down the side aisle toward the shattered window where he had found Ambriel. The arching trees were columns of carved stone, and the dappled light that danced upon the path spilled through the windows that pierced the wall.

"I saw you looking at that book back there," he said.

"What book?"

"The one in the window of the shop. The *Wonder Book*."

She nodded.

"We had that book at home when I was growing up. My sister used to read it to me."

"Emily?"

"Yes, that's right. Emily." And for an instant he was standing again at the window, peering down through the dim shop into those achingly familiar eyes.

"Maybe someone read it to me, too. It seemed familiar somehow, but I don't remember. I get flashes, glimpses, but nothing connects. Maybe I'm just crazy."

"No, you're not. Don't say that." And he reached out and took her hand in his. She gave him a long look, and he felt a power pass through him, as though a bright light had flared up inside. He let go of her hand, and they both turned away, not knowing what to say.

The buggy was in very bad shape now. The wheel was jammed against the frame. He looked back at the channel it had churned up in the soil behind them. It was hard work pulling it. He couldn't go on like this much longer. He bent down and tried to work it away from the frame.

"I'm sorry," she said. "I shouldn't have dropped it."

"It's okay." But it wasn't really. He couldn't free the wheel and he was afraid to pull on it too hard in case he completely ruined it.

"You've been awfully good to stay with me," she said. "But you can't stay forever. You have to get back home."

"I know. I'm going to have to go soon." He glanced at his watch. It was still twelve o'clock.

Suddenly she stood up and looked toward the top of the hill that rose sharply from the side of the path.

"Listen," she said.

And then he heard it too – a light, insistent sound, like the sound of birds singing. Yet too precise for birds. More like the sound of several buggies creaking along the crest of the hill.

"What *is* that?" he said.

"I don't know."

They stood listening for a minute, then without warning she took hold of the handle of the buggy and started up the side of the hill.

"Hey, where are you going?" he shouted, but she didn't answer, so he went scrambling up through the undergrowth after her.

40

He burst through the bushes at the top of the hill and collapsed on the ground, panting. He found himself at the edge of a playground packed with children and parents. The rhythmic creaking they'd heard from the foot of the hill was the sound of swings. Ambriel was standing there beside him with the buggy. She hadn't even broken into a sweat.

A woman sat knitting at one of the benches stationed around the rim of the playground. She had a smart-looking little cloth buggy by her side, into which the end of her wool disappeared. She had obviously noticed their rather unusual entrance. As he stood up he saw her poised in mid-stitch, staring over at them. She looked a little like Gran, but her buggy was in much better shape.

He brushed himself off and followed Ambriel as she walked over and settled in the shade at the base of a tree. She had taken off her coat and spread it on the ground to sit on. The T-shirt she had on underneath was none too clean. She looked different without the coat – smaller, younger. For the first time he noticed that she had a string of leather tied around her neck. A silver pendant hung from it.

"What's that?" he said, as he sat down on the coat beside her.

"I don't know," she said, as if she too were noticing it for the first time. She took the pendant in her hand and studied it. It was in the shape of a hand. Flat, and covered on both sides in a curious writing, faint and faded with age.

"These look like the letters you were drawing in the dust at the library," he said.

"I suppose," she said, but she had already lost interest. She began to root through the pockets of her coat, emptying out all the pieces of glass she had gathered on the walk. It was quite a collection.

The old woman studied the two of them over her knitting. Her eyes widened as she watched Ambriel mound the bits of broken glass on the ground in front of her.

Charles gave the buggy wheel a closer look. He was going to have to fix it before they went one step farther. He wandered off to look for a stick. By the time he got back, Ambriel had smoothed out a small patch of soil in front of her, bounded on all sides by the lacework of tree roots that ran along the ground. She sifted through her store of glass until she found a piece that pleased her. She turned it in her hand, held it to the light, then set it down in the root frame. She did this repeatedly, fitting each new piece alongside the others, until a pattern had begun to form.

Meanwhile, he turned the buggy carefully on its side and set about trying to repair the broken wheel. He popped the cap off the end of the axle and prayed it would go on tight again when he was done. Using the stick as a wedge, he started to straighten the twisted spokes. From time to time he would slip the wheel back on the axle and give it a little spin to see if it was turning true.

Beyond the pool of shade in which they sat, the playground rang with the happy sounds of children. He worked his way slowly around the wheel, moving methodically from spoke to spoke, from hub to rim. It was close, quiet work, and a calm came upon him as he did it. He did not question the calm. He took it and savored it and surrendered to it.

Time passed, punctuated by the rhythmic creaking of the swings. He worked on the wheel; Ambriel worked on her glass; the old woman worked on her knitting. He kicked off his shoes and let his tired feet air. He had never walked so long in his life as he had this day.

At one point the old woman set aside her knitting and reached into her buggy. She brought out a waxed paper packet tied with string. He watched as she slipped off the string, carefully unwrapped the paper, and brought the sandwich it contained to her mouth. His stomach began to rumble.

He remembered the greasy bag at the bottom of the buggy. He fished it out and took a peek inside. The piece of cheese had melted in the heat and glued itself to the side of the French stick. He rescued the packet of date squares and dumped the rest. He unwrapped a window in the foil and peeked in. Date squares were a crumbly thing at the best of times, and Gran's were more crumbly than most. The walk hadn't done them a whole lot of good. It could have been the car crashing into the buggy; it could have been the things that had been tossed in on top of them; it could have been the fall from the wall. What faced him when he peeked into the packet was a shapeless wad of dates half buried under a mound of crumbs.

If it had been anything other than date squares, if he had been anything other than starving, he would have pitched the whole sad mess into the garbage. As it was, he could barely keep himself from plunging into it face-first.

Ambriel had nearly filled in the root frame with the fragments of glass. She puzzled over a piece of brown glass now that looked as if it had probably come from a broken beer bottle. Charles held out the packet of date squares to her.

"Want some?"

She peeked into the packet and shook her head.

"They're date squares," he explained. The name did not quite match the reality.

She was busy fitting the bit of broken bottle into the pattern. She shook her head again.

"I know they don't look like much," he went on, "but believe me, they're delicious."

This time she didn't bother responding. He thought about how long it must have been since she'd eaten.

"You must be starving," he said.

"No, I'm fine."

He put the open packet down on the ground between them. It sat there for a while as he went back to truing the wheel. His eyes kept going back to it. It was the most delicious-looking ruin he'd ever seen. He tried to appear as uninterested in it as she seemed to be, but every time he glanced that way he began to salivate.

"You know," he said finally, "back home, people practically kill one another over these things." The mention of home brought the memory of the phone call to Gran to his mind. It settled there briefly, but he brushed it away as he kept brushing away the fly that wanted to settle on the date squares.

"Just try a little bite," he urged her. "I'm sure you'll like them."

She picked up the packet, spread the foil flaps a little, looked closely at it, held it to her nose and sniffed it. Then she put it back down on the ground.

"I can't. Okay?"

"Can't? What do you mean? I don't understand."

"I just can't, that's all."

"But why? Tell me why."

She turned and looked at him. She looked at him a long time. Finally, as though some decision had been made on her part, she said quite simply: "If I eat, I won't get back."

"Back where?"

"Back home. If I eat I won't get back home. There, I've told you."

"But that's crazy."

"I know. But there you are."

"You're not serious. How can you say that?"

"Because I know it. I don't know how I know it. I just know it – like I know you."

And that was it. She went back to piecing her glass and would say nothing more. He folded the foil shut and dropped the date squares back into the buggy.

41

Once he'd mended the wheel as well as he could, he slid it back onto the axle and tapped the cap back in place with a stone. Ambriel gathered up her glass and poured it back into the pockets of her coat. They started walking again.

Fruit trees flanked the path they took. The trees were in bloom, and when the wind blew, a shower of pink petals floated to the ground. The buggy passed quietly through them; the wheel was in better shape than it had been in a long time.

The park was full of people celebrating the sudden arrival of spring. They strolled along the paths, lounged on the grass, played tennis on the courts, or simply sat on benches, basking in the sun. The heat here was pleasant without being stifling. He was beginning to feel a bit more human again.

Ambriel no longer wandered way ahead by herself. She ambled along beside him. She had found a partially opened bud from one of the trees, lying on the path. She studied it as they walked along. She seemed fascinated by the bloomings of things.

"Look," she said, as she peeled back the casing of the bud to reveal the flower and, furled like satin about the stem below it, the leaves. The whole couched within the narrow confines of the bud.

She looked at it with the same quiet intensity that she had looked at him in the playground. He could feel the force of that look still. His mind was awhirl with questions. Why was it that she seemed never to grow tired, never to sweat, never to become hungry? If she had refused to eat and grown noticeably weaker, that would be one thing. But he was the one who was weakening; she seemed only to grow stronger. The way she had somehow scaled the wall; the way she had so effortlessly scrambled up the steep hillside with the buggy.

And then there was the cut on her forehead. Yesterday it had been bleeding like crazy. This morning there had been a small scab. Now, most of that had flaked away – and the skin beneath was as smooth as polished marble.

They moved along the petal-strewn path. The air was laced with scent. A man with a bag full of stale bread was feeding the pigeons. The birds strutted calmly about the bench where he sat, their emerald necks shimmering in the sunlight, pecking quietly at the crumbs. There were far too many crumbs for them to keep up. Bits of bread blanketed the ground around the bench. Charles found himself wishing for wings.

The path rose slowly to the crest of a hill. As they came to the top, they suddenly commanded a view of the vast park spread out in the sun like a green velvet cloth fringed about the edge with woods. And set there in the midst of all, like a crystal centerpiece on a Sunday table, stood a building all of glass, gleaming in the sun.

A great dome crowned the center of it, with smaller domes set to either side. It was like a vision, a fairy palace carefully cut from one of the colored plates in the *Wonder Book* and set down here at the heart of Caledon.

They stood for a moment, unmoving – as though moving might mar the vision – and then she turned to him and smiled.

As they came closer, the vision took on substance and soon resolved itself into a structure of glass and steel and stone. As it did so, it dawned on Charles that he knew the building. It was the Caledon Conservatory. Once, years ago, while he was staying the weekend with Gran, she had taken him to see an Easter floral display there. He remembered having been far less interested in looking at the flowers than in marveling at the intricate web of glass and steel spun high above them.

They were approaching the building from the rear. The path neared it, then veered sharply to the left and wound itself in a wide arc round to the front. As they came around to the side, Charles glanced up and was startled to see a figure perched high up on the central dome, like a spider couched at the center of its web.

He cupped his hands about his eyes to cut the glare and looked again. He saw now that there was a ladder fixed against the outer wall of the dome, shaped so as to hug the line of the dome from base to crown. A man in coveralls was stationed halfway up the ladder. In his hand, he held a long wand. One end of the wand was attached to a hose that ran down behind him to the base of the dome and into a large metal canister. He was waving the wand in a rhythmic motion, back and forth. A fine white spray fanned in a wide arc from the end of it and showered down onto the glass of the dome.

"What's he doing?" asked Ambriel.

"He's whitewashing the glass," Charles said. He had seen Gran do the same thing to the glass of her greenhouse at home. "The summer sun is too strong. You stain the glass to mute the light. And in the fall, you wash it off again."

The ladder ran along a track. A second workman was stationed at the foot of it. As his partner finished one section of the dome, he slid the ladder along to the next.

Charles craned his neck to watch them as he neared the entrance. They climbed the shallow steps. Ambriel held open the heavy wooden door and he went in with the buggy. It was as though they had crossed into another country. The air was sodden, laced with the scent of damp soil and the lush perfume of tropical plants. Giant palms rose up almost as high as the roof of the dome. He could see the shadow of the workman through the whitewashed glass. The movement of his arm back and forth reminded him of something. And he remembered the shadow of the caretaker's arm against the stained glass yesterday.

Lush vines wound along the inner walls of the building. Narrow flagstone paths, damp with the moisture that hung palpably in the air, threaded off through the greenery. They walked in single file – she in the lead, he following, negotiating the buggy along the narrow path.

Four doors opened off the central dome – to the north, to the south, to the east, and to the west. Each door opened onto another greenhouse; each greenhouse mimicked a different climate; each climate supported its unique varieties of plants.

They passed from house to house, weaving slowly along the paths, encountering wonders at every turn. From time to time, they came upon other visitors. He would turn the buggy sideways to let them by. From door to door, from house to house they passed. From regions hot and dry, where exotic succulents and giant cacti grew from the parched soil; through tropical climates, hot and damp, where orchids and hibiscuses, jade plants and begonias and lush fruit trees flourished. There were plants with elaborate pendant flowers like chandeliers, others with enormous blooms like trumpets, sounding with scent. Ambriel moved from one to another, reaching up to gently touch the delicate blooms, craning her neck to drink in the deep perfume.

Finally they passed through the fourth, the northern door, and found themselves suddenly in a house that felt like home. It was like a day at the height of summer in Caledon, caught and bottled. It was warm but not humid, and the air was full of familiar scents. He glanced about and felt he could have been standing in Gran's garden on an August day.

The path was edged with moss-covered stones and creeping thyme. Lily of the valley perfumed the shade beneath the delicate fronds of ferns. From a bed of ivy and heart-leafed hosta, there rose majestic spikes of pink-and-white foxglove, sapphire-colored delphiniums, scarlet larkspur, coralbells, and columbine. There were stands of orange daylilies and salmon-colored poppies bending beneath the weight of their blooms. Clematis and wisteria vines, laden with pink-and-purple flowers, twined up wooden trellises and wound along the glassy walls.

The path wound as well. At each turn, Charles expected to come upon Gran sitting on her little gardening stool, in her broad-brimmed straw hat, tending the beds. Instead, at the far end of the room as they rounded a bend, they found themselves before a small pond bordered with white begonias. On a mossy stone at the center of the pond, there stood a bronze statue of a girl tipping water in a steady trickle from an urn into the pond. Several large goldfish swam lazily through the crystal water. The bottom of the pond was strewn with coins, glinting up through the reflection of the glass roof that rippled on the surface of the water.

Standing beside the girl on the island, there was a swan. Its bronze wings were spread, as though it had just alighted. One wing brushed lightly against the girl's leg, and it had arched its graceful neck to gaze up at her. She, in turn, was looking down at it. They seemed poised on the brink of speech. Something in the scene struck a dim chord. As he watched the water trickle into the pond, Charles tried to plumb the riddle of the look that passed between the pair.

Ambriel had reached into her pocket and taken out a bit of amber-colored glass. She closed her eyes and tossed the piece of glass into the pool. The fish scattered as the glass fell to the bottom among the coins.

"What are you doing?"

"Making a wish," she said.

"What are you wishing for?"

"If I tell you, it won't come true."

Ripples flowed out from the spot where the glass had broken the surface of the pond; a series of circles rode out to the edge. He watched them and was suddenly reminded of the floor of the rotunda in the library, of them standing there and Ambriel craning back her neck to look up at the dome, of the way her cry had echoed through the caverned space.

On the side of the path opposite the pond, there was a wrought iron bench. She went over and sat down. He parked the buggy by the bench and sat down beside her.

There was a stillness over all. People came and went. Workers passed, pushing wheelbarrows laden with rakes and hoes, trailing hoses behind them like snakes slithering along the flagstones. Yet still there was a stillness. He could feel it down to the marrow of his bones – the steady trickle of the water, the rings riding silently outward from nave to rim, all the many blooms around them opening from their tightly clustered buds. And the two of them sitting there under the whitewashed dome at the center of the park, at the heart of Caledon.

She turned and looked at him. There had always been that odd connection between his sister Elizabeth and himself, the flow of wordless talk between them. This was like that, only more so. Something seemed to open in her eyes, like a window that had been shuttered closed. And he was suddenly aware of the eyes behind the eyes, peering through.

And at the same moment, and with the same intensity, he was aware that his interiors were open to her, that she was able to enter into him. It was as if a crystal bridge had been spun across the chasm between them. He could feel the vibrations of her footsteps as she crossed over. He could hear the telling creak as she quietly ascended the stairs of him, could hear the light complaint of hinges as she opened doors, could feel her ghostly footsteps as she descended to the cellar of him and moved among the maze of boxes there. He could sense her quietly lifting the flaps, curiously sifting through the things they had so carefully shut away.

42

Death had taken them all by surprise. They had been moving quietly along the road of life, and suddenly the ground had fallen away. He had imagined they were immortal. He had been wrong.

It was six months after the depot fire that his father had the first heart attack. A minor attack. The doctor had told him to take it as a warning. He should change his diet, slow down, not brood so much about the loss of the depot.

A new fragility crept into their lives. In less than a year, it was shattered by the second attack. And his father was dead. It was impossible. One moment they were all together, and the next he was gone.

In the days immediately following his death, they moved about as in a dream – empty, numb. The ground had grown suddenly brittle; they stepped lightly lest it shatter. The substance had fled things; only the shells remained, stretched taut over – nothing.

They had come into a dark country to which they lacked the language. They spoke, but said nothing; heard voices, but the meaning had dropped out. Cracks in the wall had widened into chasms. Pieces of the floor had fallen away. They pretended not to notice.

And through it all, through the wake, the funeral, the dreadful days and weeks that followed, while all the world about him wept, he had found himself utterly unable to cry. Something deep inside him had gone dark, and he had fled outside himself. He saw all that happened about him as if from a distance. He observed himself observing, observed others observing him. He seemed the same Charles, but everything had changed; it was the same house, but the house was haunted.

When he thought back on those days now, it was a smell that came first to mind – the smell of smoke. Since the day of the depot fire, the half dozen display cases salvaged from the blaze had been stored in the basement. The smell of smoke and cinders clung to them, as though the memory of the fire were sealed now beneath the glass along with the old photos and flyers and timetables and ticket stubs housed there.

But in the days and weeks that followed his father's death, the smell seemed to fill the whole house, so that he felt as though he were once again circling the sodden ruins that winter day.

He sought sanctuary in Emily's room. Her basement room had remained unchanged since she'd left home. Mother, convinced that her absence was merely temporary, had kept it so. Once a month she ran a mop around the room, dusted the desktop and the dresser, opened the stubborn window to circulate the air.

Emily had taken little when she left. The room retained the shape she had stamped upon it. So palpable was her presence that you would have sworn she had simply slipped out to the corner to mail a letter and would momentarily return.

He would go into the room, close the door, and lie across the bed. The same quilt covered it – the patches worn in places, the stitching come loose in others. He would lie there, staring up at the ceiling, running his thumb back and forth across the stitches on his baby finger, and feeling all the pieces of himself also coming apart.

Once, a lifetime ago, he had been happy here. He thought of those magical Saturday mornings, the two of them quietly spinning gold while the house slept. Where were those days now? What had shattered that spell and left him lying here? He ran his eyes about the room, over the familiar titles of books on the shelves, the intricate montage of pictures taped to the wall. But all was exteriors, all was surfaces: an elaborate hieroglyph he could no longer decipher, an impossible riddle for which he lacked the key.

He wished Emily were here to unlock it for him. He had never missed her more than he missed her now. Yet she was somewhere off on the other side of the country, traveling from town to town up along the coast and into the interior, working odd jobs to make enough money to move on to the next place, never setting down roots, never lingering in any one place for long: the pattern she had followed since graduating from college. Periodically, a postcard would arrive – on one side a majestic view of mountains against a crystal sky, on the other a paragraph in her minute, impossible scrawl. Less frequently there would be a letter – a page or two so tightly written you almost needed a magnifying glass to puzzle it out. Mother would look at them and moan. He quickly became the official translator.

It was more than a month after Father's death before they received a postcard with her current address and were able to reach her with the news. A rare phone call from her followed. Between tears, she talked about returning home as soon as she was able. But she never did.

Meanwhile, the four of them continued living in the house. Slowly they began to piece things together again. Smiles that had disappeared from their faces began to reappear, like the first tentative blooms of spring. They fitted the fragments together, glued them in place; bit by bit they began to mend their broken worlds. From a distance, a stranger might have had a hard time telling there was a difference. But up close you could see the cracks, like quelled lightning, running through their lives.

There were things they did not talk about because they didn't know how, didn't know where to start, didn't want to cause one another pain. There was a space between words that had not been there before. They jumped from word to word like someone crossing a stream in spring, bounding from rock to rock across the rushing water. They sprang from sentence to sentence as one leaps from rooftop to rooftop, not daring to look down.

Sometimes the space widened, sometimes narrowed, but it was always there: the way from one word to the next uncertain; the way from one sentence to the next fraught with danger. Everywhere there were fissures that had not been there before. It was no one's fault. They did the best they could.

In the midst of this, more pressing problems arose. What would they live on now with Father gone? How would they survive? Mother had always been the one at home with the children. She would need to look for work, but the money she could make would not be great. Somehow they would manage to scrape by.

It was then that Gran had suggested that they move in with her. Since Grandfather's death she had lived alone, but she was finding it more and more difficult to manage on her own. There was more than enough room for all of them in the old house. It would be the perfect arrangement for everyone.

And so, barely three months after Father's death, they had sold the bungalow, packed up their things, and moved in with Gran. That had been nearly two years ago. It felt like yesterday.

They tried to put the past behind them, tried not to dwell on it, tried to get on with their lives. But there were always the boxes, always the shadows. And through it all, he was constantly aware that he was living somewhere on the surface of himself, that something at the heart of him had gone dark since that dreadful day.

Now here was this girl, moving about among the boxes, disturbing the dust that had settled over the inner chambers of him, shredding the intricate webs that had been spun in the shadows of him.

All this passed between them in a matter of a moment, tucked between one heartbeat and the next. Not a word was spoken, yet everything was said. He turned from her, and once again they were two. He wondered if he had imagined it all.

He sat on the bench and stared at the statue of the girl pouring her endless stream of water into the pond, and he could feel the tears welling up in his eyes. He tried to force them back. He put his teeth to his sore lip and bit down till the pain of it made him wince, but the tears refused to return to where they had lain, dark and still inside him. He stared dead ahead until he could no longer see through the film of them. He blinked then and they began to trickle down his cheek, collecting at his chin until finally a drop formed, which fell to the floor between his feet.

He continued to look dead ahead – at the girl, at the swan, at the endless stream of water. He yawned, stretched, and used the opportunity to wipe his eyes. If Ambriel looked his way she would be able to tell instantly that he had been crying, just as he had always been able to tell in the dark days when Mother had been off crying by herself. He wondered now if it might not have been better for them all if they had just sat down together and bawled.

The tears kept coming. He tried not to feed them, but now that they had started, there was nothing he could do.

Then a hitch crept into his breath and a lump formed in his throat and, without warning, he began to sob. She noticed that all right. She turned and looked at him.

"You're crying," she said. "Ah, don't cry." And she put her arms about him and gathered him to her. He closed his eyes and felt as if he could lose himself in those arms forever. They were his father's arms, sweeping him up off the ground where he had fallen; his mother's arms, rocking him slowly to sleep when he was sick. They were Emily's arms, comforting him after he had caught his finger in the clock. They were all the arms that had ever gathered him in their embrace. And he cried all the tears he had ever cried. His body shook helplessly with sobs, his chest heaved, and the tears flowed like water tipped from a bottomless urn.

He had no idea how long it went on. He was aware of the shuffle of feet on the flagstones as people passed. At one point he heard a child's voice, and he opened his eyes to see a little girl standing by the pond, peering over her shoulder at the two of them as she tugged on her mother's arm.

"Look, Mommy, look," she said, and with a quick glance back, her mother whisked her away along the path.

What kind of lost, broken creatures she must have thought them, sitting there in their ragged clothes, wrapped in one another's arms.

At last it passed. He gathered himself together and went off to the washroom, where he splashed water on his face, wiped himself dry on the bottom of his pajama top, and ran his hands through his hair. There was an empty metal frame bolted to the cinder block wall above the sink, where a mirror should have been. It was probably just as well.

The buggy was sitting by itself beside the bench when he got back. Ambriel was nowhere in sight. He started down the path past the pond, wheeling the buggy behind him, wondering where she could have wandered off to. The path wound along for a ways, then stopped abruptly before a door that led to an adjacent greenhouse.

He peered through the glass and saw her. She was standing at the far end of the path on the other side. The wall beyond her was of glass and, in the glare of light that came through it, she appeared for an instant translucent.

He opened the door and was met with the familiar odor of lilies. Lilies were Gran's great love. She grew them in the small conservatory off the dining room, and in spring the house was filled with the scent of them.

Ambriel was standing before the bed of lilies. She turned to him and smiled as he walked up to her.

"There were lilies," she said. "I remember there were lilies."

43

Saturday afternoons when they were small, Mother used to send them off to the Palace. The Palace was a run-down rep theater not far from their home. Long after all the other theaters in Caledon had stopped screening Saturday afternoon matinees for kids, the Palace continued the tradition.

On warm days like this, there would be a sheen to Mother's skin and a faint smell of sweat about her as she bent to kiss them good-bye, warning Elizabeth and him to be good for Emily and to hold her hand when they were crossing the road.

They would always go by the back way, out through the yard and down the rutted lane. The lane was not paved then and, on summer days, it would smell of the creosote the city sprayed on it to keep the dust down. They would pass by the backs of yards whose ancient lilacs seemed to lean into the lane to look at them as they went by. And the warm air would be laced with the steel whine of cicadas, and the sky like a blue enamel bowl above them, so near you swore you could leap up and touch it with the tips of your fingers.

They would sit together in the charmed dark of the theater, with Emily between them, and be whisked away by wonder. Three hours later they would emerge into a different day, a day transformed by the interlude of dark. The light seemed more intense, the edges of things sharpened, colors intensified, smells and sounds magnified in remarkable ways. It was as if you had swept a fine film of dust from the surface of a mirror.

Coming out of the conservatory now was like that. The world seemed new and strange. They bumped the buggy down the shallow steps. There was a guy sitting on a bench, drinking from a bottle in a paper bag. He noticed them right away, and as they approached he held out his hat to ask for change.

Ambriel stopped and started fishing around in her coat pockets. She came out with a handful of glass. The guy watched her closely as she sifted through it. She found a bit she liked and dropped it into the hat. She gave him a big smile, turned, and started walking again.

The guy took the piece of glass out of his hat, looked at it closely, turned it in his hand, then tossed it over his shoulder onto the grass.

"Crazy chick," he muttered, as he clapped his hat back onto his head and took another drink from the paper bag.

The path was webbed with the shadows of branches. The drifts of fallen petals made it look as though the shadows themselves had come to bloom. Ambriel pulled the buggy with him as they walked along.

He felt like a bit of an idiot now for having cried like that, but she said nothing further about it. He began to wonder if she had, in fact, seen into him as he had imagined she had. One minute she would give you this look all full of knowing, and the next she would be giving a beggar a bit of broken glass. She was like this path they were walking – islands of light set in oceans of shadow.

Still, there was definitely something different about her since the conservatory. It was as though some stop in her mind had fallen away. She spoke more than she had. But the more she spoke, the stranger she seemed. It wasn't just the way she spoke – the way her words came out all wrapped and ribboned. It was the things she said.

"I don't think I come from here."

"Oh?"

"I think I come from another world."

"You can say that again."

"Not from here," she went on.

"Right."

"But from someplace inside here."

"Oh, I see, not from *here*, but someplace inside here."

"Yes, that's it."

"The trouble is, Ambriel, I don't understand what I just said."

"Suppose," she said, "that inside this world we're walking in now there is another world, occupying the same place, but invisible to this. Say that, somehow, this spilled out of that."

He nodded as if he knew what she were talking about.

"There would be passageways then," she went on, "openings between the two. Anything could be an opening, however large, however small. That dandelion there, that bird on the branch, you here – anything could be an opening of that world into this. Well, I feel as if I've somehow fallen through one of them, and I have to find the way back."

"Do me a favor, Ambriel. Don't say this to anyone else. You start talking like this and they'll put you in one of those little padded rooms and lose the key."

He glanced at his watch. It was twelve o'clock. Always. Suddenly the path they were on broke from the shelter of the trees. They found themselves at the top of a high grassy hill. Off in the distance he could see the long narrow pond that rimmed the western edge of the park. Local lore held that the pond was bottomless. Beyond the pond, riding the crest of a ridge, was a set of tracks. He looked at them and knew them instantly. In his mind he could follow the sweep of them through town, starting at the docks in the south, then forming a smooth arc as they swept north past the pond. If you followed them farther, they branched – one line skirted the stockyards and met up with the main line, while the other ran past the high wooden fence at the side of Gran's house.

Home. It was like a dream he had once had.

⁂

Ambriel had taken her guitar from the buggy and settled with it on the side of the hill. He sat beside her on the grass in the sunlight.

At the base of the hill there was a formal garden – rose beds laid out in rows around a series of reflecting pools, empty now, and, centering all, a large circular flower bed. The soil of the bed had been freshly turned. Ranged on the ground around it were dozens of flats of flowers, grouped according to color.

Rising from the center of the bed there was a curious wedge of metal, like the fin of a giant shark swimming beneath the soil. A plank of wood, resting on a wooden sawhorse at either end, spanned the bed, elevated above the soil.

A worker was poised midway along the plank, another at the edge of the bed. With a chalked line set taut between them, they marked out a pattern in the dark soil. Once the pattern was set, they began the planting. One worked from the center, the plants ranged along the plank beside her as she leaned down and set them one by one in the soil. The other worked from the edge.

As Charles sat by Ambriel's side, he watched the pattern slowly take form. The sun reflected off the still water of the pond. A flock of gulls wheeled and swooped. Ambriel tuned the guitar and began to play. She played very lightly, very softly, like someone whispering to herself. He had to strain to hear.

She would start up a piece, take it along a little, then stop suddenly, go back, and start up again. It was as if she was trying to remember how it went. Each time she started it up again, she took it along a little farther. She played it over so often that the tune got stuck in his head. He closed his eyes and pictured his fingers picking out the notes on the piano as she played.

And then suddenly it soared. Like a bird abandoning the earth, it leapt up into light. It caught an invisible current of air and looped, soared, swam. There was no effort, no strain. It was pure, simple, perfect. The same pattern of notes repeated, but with infinite variation, as though each time it came around again she discovered another unsuspected facet of it, a new passage through it. So that finally, when she floated back to the bare theme, sewn into the simple statement now was all the hidden wealth of the variations.

He had never heard anything like it. It was more like thinking than like music – like thinking through music. And the thought seemed to flow through all, seemed to knit the whole into the one harmony. It flowed through him as well, so that, while it played, he felt a stillness settle over him and a deep peace pervade him. And, for a moment, he was the music.

She finished playing and sat very still with the guitar resting across her knees. He glanced down the hill and was shocked to find that most of the pattern had been filled in. Ambriel's playing seemed to have lasted mere minutes, yet time had somehow sped past.

The pattern of blooms was now apparent. The circle was divided into quadrants. At the line dividing each, there was a Roman numeral fashioned out of flowers. The fin of steel he had seen rising from the soil cast its shadow across the pattern. It was a sundial. And the shadow fell across the three.

It was impossible. It couldn't be three o'clock. He scrambled to his feet and raced up the hill to the path. He asked the time of the first person who passed. It was after three. He had been blissfully unaware of time passing, but now it washed over him in a chill wave. If he'd known what time it was, he would have left long ago. Gran would be mad with worry. He couldn't wait any longer. He had to get back home.

He returned to the spot where they had been sitting.

"I have to go," he told her.

"I know," she said.

"I feel bad about leaving you, but I just have to get back home."

"I understand."

"I should have been home ages ago."

"I understand."

"Look, will you stop being so understanding. There's nothing I can do. I have to get back."

"I under – Sorry."

His eyes drifted back to the set of tracks riding the ridge on the far side of the pond. If he followed the line, he could cut the time getting home in half.

"Will you be all right?" he asked her.

"I'll be fine."

He felt like a real creep, leaving her there like that.

"Well, good luck," he said, and held out his hand for her to shake.

It was a stupid thing to do. She looked at it a moment, like she wasn't sure what to do with it. Then she reached up and took the pendant on the leather string from around her neck and put it in his hand.

"Thank you," she said, and she folded his fingers over it.

He was ready to start crying all over again. But there wasn't time for that now. He put the pendant in his pocket, then took the buggy and started up the hill.

When he got to the top he turned to wave, but she was looking off the other way. She looked small and lone and ragged sitting there on the clipped grass, like a weed the gardener had overlooked. He waited a minute, hoping she might turn. He thought of calling out, but didn't.

The distance had already done its work. He turned and started walking away as quickly as his legs would carry him.

44

He tried to block from his mind how bad he felt, but with each turn of the wheel the buggy seemed to whisper, *Creeep. Creeep.* He spotted a phone booth by a clutch of benches. He patted his pockets, hoping that by some miracle a quarter might have materialized there, so that he could call home.

Close by the phone booth, a paper box stood chained to a pole. He sidled over to it and was about to check the change box, when a woman appeared on the path with her dog. He bent down as if to read the headline on the paper until she went past, then he reached out and tucked his finger into the change slot. Empty. He pumped the coin return button a couple of times, gave the door a little yank, gave the box a little shake. It refused to cough up so much as a slug. He kicked it once for good measure while he went through his pockets again.

He went over and checked the change slot on the pay phone. Empty. He banged the receiver up and down a couple of times, then happened to glance up. Tucked in the shade of a tree on the other side of the path, sucking back a drink from a water bottle, there was a cop on a bike.

He set the receiver down as gently as if he were laying a baby in its cradle. He took hold of the buggy and started walking slowly down the path, hoping against hope that the cop somehow had not seen him. His heart was pounding in his chest like a sledgehammer. He thought about the *Name Your Baby* book in the bottom of the buggy, and his legs went liquid. He was ready to puddle down onto the path.

Just as he had begun to think that he had escaped, the cop slid up beside him on the bike.

"Hang on there a minute, fella."

The cop pulled in front of him and got off the bike. He was well over six feet tall. He took off his helmet and hung it from the handlebars. He was wearing dark shades. Charles saw himself mirrored in them as the cop stood in front of him. He had pulled a notebook and pen out of his pocket.

"Where are you off to, young man?"

"Home."

"And where's home?"

Charles blurted out his old address. It was the first thing that came into his head. It was already said before he realized it was wrong, and then it was too late to unsay it. The cop gave him a long look, then looked past him at the buggy.

"What's your name, son?"

"Eliot." This was not a particularly bright thing to do, lying to a cop.

"What happened to your lip, Eliot?"

"I fell."

"I see." He ran his eyes over the bloody pajama top. Charles had a sinking feeling he wasn't buying any of this.

"Do you work, Eliot?"

"I have a paper route."

"A paper route? Kind of old for that, aren't you?"

He let that one go.

The cop was eyeing the buggy now. "What have you got in there, Eliot?"

"Just my jacket and stuff."

The cop fished a long arm into the buggy. He rifled around in the bottom of it a bit. He picked up the *Name Your Baby* book, flipped through it, put it back. He came out with the foil pack like he'd just scored something big. Charles watched him unwrap it and peek in. He poked at the powder with his finger.

"Date squares," said Charles.

The cop was not amused. He squished the pack closed and dropped it back into the buggy. He looked at Charles.

"Listen to me, Eliot. Next time I catch you abusing private property like you were back there, I'm going to take you down to the station. You understand me?"

"Yes, sir."

"You move along now."

"Yes, sir."

After the cop had cycled safely out of sight, Charles began thinking of all the things he ought to have said. He worked that up for a while as he walked along; then suddenly he pictured the possibility of the cop running into

Ambriel. He didn't like the thought of how that would play out. Ambriel was utterly guileless; she was apt to say just about anything. Two minutes of talking to her and the cop would have her clapped into the bughouse with all the other crazies.

He stopped dead, stood there for a couple of minutes wrestling with his conscience, gave up, and began walking back to where he'd left her.

45

She was not there. There was no sign of her on the hillside, or anywhere near it. He walked around in circles awhile, but it was useless; she could have headed off in any number of directions. He had just about given up, when off in the distance he heard a sound – a faint, familiar whistle. He followed it and soon found himself at the foot of a hill, where a popcorn vendor had stationed his cart.

A shiver passed through him. He was standing at the entrance to the zoo he had dreamt about last night.

People were gathered about the animal pens set to either side of the steep road that ran up the hill. There were buffalo and llamas, musk oxen and Barbary sheep; children pushed carrots and celery stalks through the fence for deer to nibble; mountain goats stood perched on rocky ledges and dreamt of distant peaks.

And the high thin whistle of the popcorn cart threaded through all. Charles looked up toward the crest of the hill, and the memory of that long-ago day came hurtling down to meet him. It had been a day not at all unlike this day. It was as though Nature herself had conspired to resurrect the memory now.

A profound sense of strangeness enveloped him. The popcorn cart was hung with balloons, stuffed toys suspended from strings, plastic windmills spinning in the breeze. As he passed the colored cart, he felt as though he were going through the gateway of a dream.

He started up the hill, pulling the buggy behind him. It seemed not nearly as steep, not nearly as high as it had that day. He moved through the crowd as one invisible, striding the seam that joined one time with another, astray in the realm of spirits.

The crowd shifted and he spotted a figure, a guitar slung over one shoulder, standing halfway up the hill in front of one of the pens. The crowd flowed past her, but she remained immobile, like a stone in a stream. It was Ambriel, fallen into one of her trances as she stared into the pen. He was still too far off to see what it housed, but she was the only one bothering to stand about. Others would come up, see her standing there like that, look briefly into the pen, then pass on.

Charles stood for a moment, watching her. He was struck by her strangeness as she stood there spellbound, with her spiked hair and her tattered clothes and her coat pulled closed in the heat. If he'd been a cop, he would have stopped her for sure.

He began walking slowly up the hill toward her. She was standing so still that several sparrows had landed at her feet and were calmly pecking at the stray bits of bread that lay on the ground about the pen. They instantly took to flight as Charles walked up to her.

"Hi," he said.

She did not, of course, respond. She never did when she was like this.

The sign on the front of the pen read:

> BLUE PEAFOWL (Pavo cristatus)
> GEOGRAPHICAL DISTRIBUTION: India and Sri Lanka.
> DESCRIPTION:
> MALES: head, neck, and breast metallic blue; tail coppery green with bronze-green eyes.
> FEMALES: mainly brown with some iridescent green on neck. Both sexes have head crests.
> DIET: Seeds, fruits, insects, and plants.
> LIFESPAN: Up to fifteen years in captivity.

The pen was laid out in a series of terraces. A small log cabin crowned the highest terrace. It put him in mind of Emily's basement room in the old house. The cabin had a high conical roof, like a witch's cap. It reminded him of the depot roof. Standing by the open doorway of the enclosure was a bird with brilliant blue plumage. It had a long sinuous neck and a small head, with a delicate crest set upon it like a crown. A long train of feathers trailed to the ground behind it, blue and green and eyed like ermine. Both Ambriel and the bird were motionless. They seemed to be staring at one another, locked in some silent communion. But his coming had broken the spell; the bird looked away and began to walk up and down in front of the hut, drawing its long tail along the ground behind it.

"Charles, what are you doing here?" said Ambriel, suddenly aware of his presence. "I thought you were going home."

"I was. I just . . . I just wanted to give you this," he said, and purely on impulse, he reached into the buggy and came out with the crumpled ball of foil that contained the ruins of Gran's date squares. He smoothed it out a bit and handed it to her. "I, ah . . . I thought maybe you might want this. Later, I mean."

She looked at him, looked through him, a long moment. "Thanks," she said, taking it and putting it into her coat pocket.

She went back to watching the peacock. The bird was still pacing up and down in front of the cabin. Every now and then there would come a shrill squawk from inside, and he would catch a glimpse of a peahen, as she poked a wary head out from the shadows of the hut.

While some of the other creatures hung about the fence, looking for handouts, the peacock kept as far from the crowd as it possibly could. The sign said that it had come originally from India. It was a long way from India to Caledon and, as the bird paced the narrow confines of its prison like a king in exile, trailing his splendor through the dirt, it looked as if it would have been a good deal happier to be home.

As they stood there, a constant procession of people, working their way from one pen to the next, would pause before the peacock pen, look briefly at the bird off pacing in the distance, and move on to more promising fare.

Occasionally, someone would steal a glance over in their direction as if to ask, "What exactly are you looking at?"

He was beginning to wonder the same thing himself.

"What will you do tonight?" he asked Ambriel.

"Don't know. Stay here maybe." She glanced up at the sky. "There'll be stars tonight," she said.

There was another long space of silence. He looked up over his shoulder at the crest of the hill. He kept expecting to see the cop on the bike appear there.

"Look," he said, "maybe you could come home with me." As soon as he said the words, he realized that that was why he'd really returned. All the while he'd been wandering around looking for her, the decision had been taking shape inside.

Few things seemed to take her by surprise. But his invitation home seemed to have. She gave him a long look, then quickly turned away. There was a sheen to her eyes, as though she was on the point of tears.

"What if everything is happening everywhere at once?" she said, as if it were somehow a response to his invitation.

"Is that a yes or a no?" he asked.

The high, thin whistle of the popcorn cart had suddenly intensified, detaching itself from the texture of surrounding sounds. He turned and saw that the vendor had left his place at the entrance to the zoo and was starting up the hill, pushing the cart ahead of him. All you could see of him were his feet; the rest of him was hidden behind the cart as he labored it up the steep incline.

The sight of the cart on the hill struck a chord deep inside Charles. He stared at it a moment, then turned back to the peacock pen. The other bird had appeared at the entrance of the hut. It too wore a crown, but its dress was of a duller hue and it had no train. As it emerged into the light, the peacock stopped its pacing. Suddenly it raised its dusty train from the ground and fanned it open. And instantly there appeared a brilliant wheel of color, full of eyes, framing the bird.

The beauty of it knocked the breath out of him. It was as though this bird, dragging its tail through the dust of its cage, had suddenly recalled its true nature. The wheel of feathers shimmered in the sunlight; it seemed to turn in its stillness, and the many colors blended into the one brilliance, and the eyes were like windows in the wheel.

A gasp went up from those standing before the pen. A dog barked. A bottle slipped from the hands of a startled child. Charles watched it fall. It seemed to fall forever, so that he could study the glint of sun off the glass, watch the liquid flung like waves against the inner side. Then it struck the pavement and shattered. And the sound of its shattering was the final piece of a puzzle falling into place.

He swung his gaze again to the crest of the hill. In the bright light he saw a boy on a tricycle, poised there. The breaking of the bottle had startled the boy. Charles watched and, at the same time, felt the boy's feet leave the ground – and the wheels of the tricycle begin to turn.

For an instant that widened into eternity, the boy's gaze settled on him. He read the shock registered there and felt the fear like a taste on his tongue.

The tricycle picked up speed as it started down the hill. Charles stood rooted to the spot – watching, telling himself all the while that what he was seeing could not be real, that somehow the memory of that day had been drawn up from the depths of him by the dream and been spilled out here on the hill. He was here, standing by Ambriel in front of the peacock pen. He could feel the handle of the buggy in his palm. He could feel the ache of his feet. He could feel the slight throb of his battered lip, the prickle of the heat on his back, the dull knot of hunger in his empty belly. He was here. That other him, starting down the hill on the tricycle, was a dream, an illusion, a figment of his fevered imagination, the result of too much sun and too little food.

And yet it was real – so real that he could see the spokes of the wheel whirl into a blur as the tricycle picked up speed. He stood there spellbound, knowing with dread how the scene would inevitably unfold. He watched the trike thread its way through the people in its path. Some seemed not to notice as it sped past them; others stepped aside and turned their heads to follow its course down the hill.

The whole scene was wrapped in silence. Even the steady whistle of the popcorn cart inching its way up the hill had been quenched by it. Time had utterly fallen away. He watched himself hurtling down the hill. And the same terror froze his hands to the buggy handle as froze the boy's hands to the handlebars of the tricycle. He saw the boy's mouth fall open in horror as the popcorn cart loomed up inescapably in his path. And the wail that shattered the silence seemed to spill from both their mouths as one.

And then, from out of nowhere, a figure darted onto the roadway; so fast did it move that the flaps of its coat flew out behind it like wings. As the tricycle careened out of control, the figure plucked the boy free of it and seemed to fly through the air with him in its arms, over the tricycle as it crashed into the curb, and onto the grassy verge by the roadway.

For a long moment the two lay side by side, wound in one another's arms. And then, like a fog of breath fades slowly from a windowpane, the figure faded, then vanished. And there was only the boy lying motionless on the grass. He watched him stir, saw the eyes flutter open and briefly meet his through the turning wheel of the trike.

For one mad moment he thought that the figure he had seen dart onto the roadway had been Ambriel, but when he turned to her now, he found her still staring into the peacock pen. He turned back to the boy, but at that moment the popcorn cart, continuing its progress up the hill, had come between them, blocking his view. He watched the large wheels slowly turn, heard the shrill whistle as the steady plume of steam ascended and dissolved in the air.

As it passed, it took the moment with it in its wake. For when he looked again at the place where the boy had been, not a remnant of the incident remained. No boy, no bike, only a quiet spot of grass by the side of the road.

He stared at it in wonder, like one awakened from a dream. As he turned back to the pen, the peacock slowly folded its fan of feathers closed and lowered its train down to the dirt.

Ambriel turned to him and smiled.

"I guess we'd better be going," she said. She hooked her hand beside his on the handle of the buggy, and they started together down the path and out of the park.

46

Two sets of tracks ran side by side. One set gleamed in the sunlight as it slid off into the distance; the other slunk along beside it, its rails coated in rust, weeds springing between the rotting ties. By summer's end, the rusted track would be all but hidden beneath a crazy quilt of goat's-beard, blueweed, bladder campion, and Queen Anne's lace.

Charles walked along the abandoned track, bumping the buggy along behind him over the ties. It was awkward walking. The space between ties was too short for a proper stride, yet to skip one and stride to the next was too far a stretch. He was left hobbling along in half steps, having to think about each step he took.

The city showed its hind parts to the tracks: dump sites, scrap yards, timeworn buildings in graffiti gowns, tired houses hunched behind tumbledown fences. But then, for a stretch, the track would seem to shake itself free of the city. Bushes would spring high to either side; birdsong would fill the air. And looking down the length of track, you would swear you had suddenly been spirited into the countryside.

Ambriel meandered along beside him, stooping to study the weeds, snaring bits of broken glass from the gravel of the roadbed. The way the late afternoon sun struck the scattered glass made it look as if a trail of jewels had been strewn along the track. The broken trail they had been following all day through Caledon was now leading them home.

Home. The word sounded strange. He felt as if he'd been away for years. Would Gran recognize him when he came to the door? Or would they have to split the seams of their coats and scatter their jewels on the ground before she remembered who he was?

He was bone tired. Every muscle in his body ached. His mouth was parched. His lip was sore. His face felt baked. His eyes burned. He wanted to run down the line now that they were so near home, but he was forced to hobble along from tie to tie, like a toddler learning to walk.

Walking the track in the heat was hypnotic. He painted the scene of his homecoming on the repeating pattern of ties. He pictured Gran opening the door, pictured her flinging her arms about him. He would tell her everything and she would understand, and he would meld back into the life before as seamlessly as if he'd never left it.

The reality lay elsewhere. The wager of this endless day had altered all. The home he returned to would not be the home he had left. He could not go back, he could only go on.

He knew Gran well enough to know that his phone call that morning would have been niggling at her all day. He could imagine her irritation at missing her hair appointment inching cautiously toward concern as time passed and he did not appear. Still, the first emotion she would display when he finally did appear would be anger. He would have to explain where he had been, the state he was in, why he had let her down. He didn't know whether he could explain it to himself, much less to her.

He rehearsed what he would say, trying first this tack then that, working slantwise toward the truth. Suddenly he stopped short, startled by the sound of his voice, and realized he'd been talking aloud to himself as he walked along the track. He looked down at himself, his pajama top all stained and sweaty, the steam engine still just emerging from the dark of the tunnel.

The foreground of faded rails in the picture seemed to merge now with the rusted rails he walked along. It was as though the ancient engine had broken from its brief darkness to ride this rusty stretch of track that took him home.

As he stood looking down, he spotted a glint of amber glass all but buried beneath the gravel. He slowly worked the stones away with the toe of his shoe, then bent down and rooted out the glass from its resting place. Lord, he was getting to be just as crazy as she was.

It was old glass, much thicker than any of the glass he'd seen Ambriel gather that day. One edge of it was arced, as if the piece were part of the base of a bottle. He wondered how long it had been lying there. Likely a long while. He wiped it clean on the sleeve of his shirt and held it to the light. And up from the amber depths of it there rose a memory – the memory of the morning Elizabeth and he had barricaded themselves in the cold room.

They could have been no more than four. The two of them had tiptoed downstairs while the rest of the family was still fast asleep. They had hoped that Emily might be awake, but her door was closed and the crack beneath the door was dark, so they turned their attention elsewhere.

Tucked in the space between the workbench and the underside of the stairs, cloaked in a plastic drop sheet to ward off the dust and discourage small intruders, was Father's pride and joy – an elaborate model train layout depicting the town of Caledon in the golden age of the steam engine. Model trains had been a passion with him since he was a boy. The layout was the labor of years, a scale model of the town and the surrounding countryside meticulously fashioned from papier-mâché and paint. There were balsa wood buildings lining the main street; a model of the depot, complete with conical roof. There were trees made from twigs from the lilac bush out back, with green foam for foliage. There were miniature wooden people standing on the platform of the depot. There were baggage carts, a horse and wagon; and in the rolling fields beyond the town, plaster cows grazed contentedly on the painted grass. And running through all, like a web spun over the landscape, were the twin lines of the Niagara Northwestern.

The temptation was too great. They lifted the plastic drop sheet and let it fall with a soft *swish* to the floor. For a while they simply stood, simply looked; then they moved the horse and wagon quietly along the sleeping street, paced the people up and down the platform as they waited for their train. The trains themselves stood as still as the cattle in the field. One had halted halfway through a turn; the other was tucked inside a tunnel cut through one of the hills on the outskirts of town.

They flicked a switch and the engines jerked into life. As they rattled along the track, the landscape woke in their wake. The train pulled up to the depot; people boarded and disboarded; luggage was taken off and loaded on, and the train went on its way.

Time passed, and still the house slept about them. As they grew weary of the game, they grew more daring. The trains picked up speed. There were several near derailments, several near collisions where the trains crossed paths. Finally, one of them decided it might be a neat idea to block one end of the tunnel with cows and see what would happen when the train came through. Their four-year-old eyes were wide with anticipation as the train roared around the track and disappeared into the tunnel. There was a momentary silence, then the cows exploded from the end of the tunnel. The train emerged, jumped the track, and went flying off the layout, landing with a loud crash against the side of the furnace. One of the cows fell onto the track. The other train plowed into it, jumped the rail, and slammed into the side of the depot platform, injuring several wooden people.

Through their shock at the scene before them, they heard the sound of Father's footsteps hurrying across the floor overhead. They ran and barricaded themselves in the cold room.

They heard him come down the stairs, heard him pick the train up off the floor, flick off the power to the layout.

He didn't say a word. For the remainder of that morning, the two of them shut themselves in the cold room amid the shelves of jars and tins and the broken things that Father would one day fix, while piece by piece he dismantled the layout and moved it out to the garage.

Later, they were all able to laugh about it. The story of the day the twins barricaded themselves in the cold room became part of the Endicott family lore. But as Charles stood on the track now, looking down at the piece of glass in his hand, it was the silence of that morning he remembered most – the vast silence that surrounded his father as he dismantled the layout, the silence that sat with them in the cold room like an unseen presence.

That day was not gone. It was present still in memory. He could no more shut it away than he could plug the tunnel against the oncoming train. It was part of him – part of the pattern of moments that made him. If he closed his eyes, the stillness now was the stillness then, was the stillness of that morning they had pulled their sleds through the snowbound world, was the stillness of those stolen hours in the empty church, was the stillness of this strange girl gathering glass along the track.

They were getting close to home. He was beginning to recognize landmarks along the way: the backs of familiar buildings, the set of signal lights he could see from his room; finally, the high weatherworn fence that bordered the backyard, and the housetop peeking above it.

"We're here," he said to Ambriel, as he stepped off the track and waded through the weeds to the fence. She came over and stood beside him as he slid back the loose board and looked into the empty yard. His eyes fell on the shed, and he had a sudden idea.

"Listen," he said, "maybe it would be best if I was to go in first alone and try to calm down my Gran a bit before I tell her about you. You could wait in the shed there, and I'll come and get you as soon as I can."

She listened, looked at the shed, then nodded in agreement. The house seemed quiet. The kitchen light was off, the back porch cast in shadow. They crept along to the shed and opened the door. He lifted Gran's gardening stool down from the nail where it hung on the wall and cleared a place for her to sit amid the clutter.

"You're sure you'll be all right here?"

"I'll be fine. Don't worry."

"I'll be back as soon as I can."

The sight of her sitting there on the little stool looking up at him as he closed the door lingered in his mind long after.

47

Mr. Berkeley looked up from his work to find that time had fled. For hours he had been patiently repiecing the figure in the glass, but try as he might, he could not make it come right. Now suddenly he realized the reason why. A piece was missing.

He left the work where it lay and hurried along the passageway and up the stairs into the church. He searched along the sill of the broken window; he searched the floor beneath the bench. But it was not to be found.

As he came back into the room, he pulled his keys from his pocket. Among the keys clustered at the end of the length of twine – the solid old keys to the doors of the church, the small brass keys to the money boxes, the random array of keys to cabinets and storage rooms – there was a small skeleton key. He took that key now and turned it in the lock of the old trunk at the foot of the bed.

The inside of the trunk was piled high with those things he had salvaged from his past. On the top there were photo albums and packets of letters tied with faded ribbon. He lifted them out and set them on the bed. Below these there was a level of clothing, smelling faintly of lilac, covered in tissue paper gone yellow with time. Lower lay a stratum of books, most of them books on glass. Indeed, the deeper he delved, the more all became glass.

The books rested on a false bottom. He pried it up now and revealed a level of swaddled things. He unfolded a few as he lifted them out. A stained glass butterfly, a rose in bud, a bird on the wing, a few abstract pieces: things the two of them had made. He had let all the larger work go. It was these trinkets he had kept, these bits of whimsy they had put together to amuse one another, all of them made with glass culled from the box of "curious" – those odd, flawed bits left over from larger work, but far too beautiful to throw away.

When everything else had shattered about him, he had kept these few things close: these trinkets, and his tools, and the box of curious. The two wooden boxes lay on the bottom of the trunk, wound about with lengths of lead. He took them out now and set about opening them for the first time since he'd set them there years before.

He sifted through the curious until he found a piece of glass that was a near match to the one that was missing. He opened the box of tools, lifted them out, and laid them on the table. Pliers for stretching the leads, a cutting knife, the stopping knife with its weighted handle for tapping the leads tight to the glass, farrier's nails, the bone lathekin for opening and smoothing the leads, soldering iron and solder, tallow for flux, a diamond wheel for cutting the glass. The very heft of them in his hand woke memories.

He marked the piece of curious, cut it to size, and set it in place in the pattern. He found his hands shaking. He looked over at the picture of his wife hanging on the wall.

"Be with me now, my love," he murmured.

He found two pieces of wood and nailed them to the table to form a right angle. He stretched two lengths of lead, cut them to size, and set them against the inner side of the frame. Then he took the corner piece from the pattern of glass he had assembled and fit it into the corner of the frame, tapping it home to the heart of the lead. He cut another strip, molded it to that, and worked the next bit of glass into the outer channel of the lead. He tapped in two nails to hold it tight while he set a neighboring piece of glass in place, cut and shaped another piece of lead, added the next piece of glass, and tapped in two more nails.

He fanned out steadily from the corner, composing the pattern piece by piece, shifting the nails outward as he went. The rhythms of the work, at first unfamiliar after so long a break, gradually wove themselves back into the motion of muscle and bone, until in time the piece seemed to flow from him with the same ease as that of a spider spinning its web.

48

The porch door slapped closed behind him. He picked the buggy up and hung it back on its hook. It felt as if years had passed since he'd lifted it down that morning. It bore the battle scars of the day. A wiry stem of bindweed had wrapped itself about the axle; bits of bloom festooned the battered frame.

GRADE A EGGS. FRAGILE. The words on the side of the sorry box so worn you could hardly make them out. He could not bear to empty the box now, lest disturbing those things that lay there might shatter the memory of the day.

The slamming of the door had alerted Gran to the fact that he was home. He could hear her calling through the house as she came.

"Charles? Is that you, Charles?"

"Yes, it's me, Gran."

"You had me worried sick, young man," she said, as she appeared in the kitchen doorway. "Do you have any idea what time it is?"

She looked over at him standing there in the shadows by the buggy. He could see her struggling with her dim eyesight to piece together the scene before her. She looked from him to the buggy and back again.

"I'm sorry I worried you, Gran," he said, as he started toward her. "I'm sorry I let you down. I lost track of time."

"Good Lord, boy, what's happened to you?"

"I fell. It's okay, I'm all right."

She took him by the hand and led him into the kitchen. She sat him down, pushed his hair back from his face, looked closely at the cut on his lip. As she ministered to him, he stared at the delicate network of lines running through her face, the light dusting of powder on her cheek; he smelled the delicate scent of lavender that drifted from her clothes. It seemed a lifetime since he'd seen and smelled these things. He drank them in deep draughts, as one who has been dying of thirst drinks water.

She ran a cloth under cold water, wiped his face, dabbed gently at the cut.

"You've got a bad burn from the sun, too. What *have* you been doing?"

"Walking," he said. "Walking and walking." Now that he was finally home, he felt a profound weariness fall upon him like a weight. He was afraid he might pitch forward off the chair onto the floor. Gran sensed the shape he was in. She rewet the cloth, folded it, laid it across the nape of his neck till the faintness passed. She did not press him with more questions.

"You go upstairs and clean yourself up," she said. "I'll fix you something to eat. We can talk later."

An oilcloth covered the dining room table. The contents of Gran's curio cabinet were ranged over it. The doors of the cabinet were open. The glass shelves gleamed. A few things had been dusted and returned to their places. The rest waited.

The house and everything in it seemed strange to him as he moved through it, as if he were seeing it after a long absence. It was as if the order of things had been slightly shifted, the relation of the parts to the whole slightly altered; his eye no longer glided over the surface of things unthinking, but was jarred at every instant by the strangeness of their being.

At the foot of the stairs, he stopped and stared at the early map of Caledon, the pattern of roads and rail lines. Halfway up the stairs, where the tread creaked, he stopped again. The subtle threads that bound one thing to another, one time to another, seemed almost palpable, as though the house were hung with webs.

The face that met him in the mirror seemed no longer his. His lip was swollen; his skin was burnt; there was that in his eyes that had not been there before. While the water ran in the tub, he stripped off his clothes. There was a light chime as something fell from his pants pocket onto the tile floor. It was the pendant Ambriel had given him in the park.

He bent and picked it up. He turned the small, inscribed hand in his and wondered again at the minute markings that covered it. He placed it around his neck and thought immediately of Ambriel sitting waiting in the shed.

He bathed quickly, pulled on some clean clothes, looked briefly from his bedroom window down into the yard. The day had begun to feel like something he had dreamed. He could not quite believe she was out there.

He hurried downstairs. Gran had fixed him a sandwich. She left him to eat in peace while she went back to work on the curio cabinet. He pushed the food mechanically into his mouth, but all the while he was eating his thoughts were with Ambriel.

He tried to force himself to think clearly, but his mind went round and round like a creaking wheel.

What was he going to do? It would soon be dark. He glanced up at the Four Quartets clock. Its measured ticking seemed to fill the room.

He wandered into the sunroom. The scent of soil and bloom laced the still air. He peeked between the thicket of plants ranged along the sill and caught a glimpse of the shed. The shadows were lengthening in the yard. Set in the wall of the shed that faced him, there was a window covered by a metal grate. He imagined a dim shape there, staring back.

He put up the lid of the piano and began to play the little Bach piece he knew by heart – the opening aria of the "Goldberg Variations." Music made in heaven, Gran called it. It whisked him back to the restaurant that morning, when the strains of it had sounded through the jukebox. But how? He was far too tired to plumb the mystery of it now. The whole day was wound in mystery, and at the heart of it stood Ambriel.

Part of him was there with her in the shed, and part of her was here with him. He felt her dance herself down through his fingers, guiding them, so that the piece he was playing was no longer the aria at all, but the piece she had played in the park. Note for note it flowed, as if it were something he could remember as readily as his name. It rose into the air, soared and swooped and swam, and at last touched lightly down. It was time. He closed the lid of the piano and went into the dining room.

"What was that piece you were playing just now?" asked Gran, looking up at him as he sat down at the end of the table.

"Just something someone taught me. A friend."

"It's very beautiful," she said.

Ranged upon the green oilcloth between them lay a field of figurines and ornaments and knickknacks of all shapes and descriptions. It was hard to believe they had all come from the curio cabinet.

As she took up each piece, she would run the dust cloth over it, and return it to its place upon the shelf. Some of the objects seemed quite precious: crystal weights, delicate porcelain figurines, objects of intricately tooled ivory and jade. Others were the normal bric-a-brac you could see in any junk shop window. They sat there together, the high and the low. The value they possessed related to the people who had once owned them, or the circumstances under which they had been obtained. They were tags to time past, and the yearly ritual of dusting them down was as much a dusting down of memory.

"Are you feeling a little better now?" Gran asked, as she picked up a crystal paperweight from the table and ran her cloth over it. The paperweights lay scattered among the other objects like islands of stillness in the landscape.

"Yes," he said, wondering where to start. He watched her turn the weight in her hand – a small sphere of glass with a pale pink rose sunk in the center.

"I found this in a little shop in London. Your grandfather and I had just been married. We were impossibly young and very much in love. It was the last day of his leave, I remember. We spent the afternoon walking along the river in the rain, sharing our one umbrella, talking about the future. We talked of the future endlessly then.

"As we were walking we happened to pass a little secondhand shop. And there in the window, surrounded by all the most dreadful trash, was this wonder. I caught sight of it out of the corner of my eye as we passed. We stopped and went back.

" 'Do you see it?' I said, as we stood there with the rain running off the umbrella. He looked at me as if I were mad, then looked back at the cluttered window.

" 'Ah, you mean that piece of glass?' he said.

" 'Yes, that piece of glass, as you put it.'

" 'Would you like it?'

" 'Yes. As a memento of the day.'

"So in we went. I can recall the inside of that shop as if it were yesterday. The dimness, the smell of dust and old wood and books. The smell the past would wear if it came to call. And there behind the counter was an old man repairing the clasp of a necklace with a pair of pincers. He looked up at us over the rim of his glasses. I'm sure we looked quite bedraggled from the rain.

"'Can I help you with something?' he asked.

"I asked him how much he wanted for the little paperweight in the window. He climbed out from behind the counter and went to fetch it, reaching in over the rest of the things, shifting this and that, stretching to lay hold of it. He brought it out, turned it over, glanced at a little label on the base.

"'Four pounds,' he said, poised there, ready to put it back, for it was a fair sum of money in those days.

"'We'll take it,' I said, perhaps a little too eagerly, for he turned it over curiously in his hand and eyed it with a questing interest as he came back to the counter.

"Your grandfather thought I was mad to pay that kind of money for a piece of glass. But between the two of us, we managed to scrape together enough to buy it.

"'Shall I wrap it?' the old man asked, as I handed him the money over the counter.

"'No, I'll just take it as it is.'

"As he handed it to me, we traded glances, and his eyes said he sensed that some rare thing had just escaped his grasp.

"We walked home through the rain under the shelter of the umbrella. In the pocket of my coat, I clutched the weight and felt the smooth coolness of it against my palm. The next day your grandfather was shipped out with his regiment. It was almost two years before we saw one another again. Nine months after he left, your father was born."

She set the weight down on the shelf of the cabinet. The rose, magnified as though by magic, seemed to fill the whole interior of the sphere.

"For months this weight will sit here among the other things on the shelf of the cabinet, and I will walk by it countless times a day and give it barely a glance. But I need merely take it down and hold it again in my hand, and the whole of that moment returns to me instantly. I hear the patter of rain; I smell the smell of wet wool and dust and old wood and books; I feel the weight of it in my hand as the shopkeeper handed it to me.

"Nothing vanishes. Not a speck or a hair passes away. It is always here, always now. There is no end to the mystery of things."

She turned to him.

"I have something to tell you, Gran," Charles said finally.

"Yes," she said, "I expect you do."

She tucked a stray wisp of hair behind her ear with her long fingers, then took off her apron and sat down in a chair at the opposite end of the table. She crossed her legs, smoothed her skirt, and sat studying him across the field of ornaments and figurines, until at last he spoke.

"Do you remember last night," he began, "when I asked you if someone who got hit on the head could lose their memory?"

"Yes, I remember."

"Well, I met someone who that happened to. A girl. A girl in a church."

"In a church? What church?"

"St. Bartholomew's."

"St. Bartholomew's. But whatever were you doing there?"

He took a deep breath. "Skipping my piano lesson."

She looked at him intently. "I'm afraid I don't understand," she said. "Perhaps you'd better begin at the beginning."

49

And so he did – with that day two months back, when he'd first decided to skip the lesson. He told her about stumbling onto St. Bartholomew's and going inside to escape the cold, then returning each Friday afterward. He told her about going there yesterday, about the breaking of the window, about finding the injured girl in the pew. He tried to give words to the emotions he felt after leaving her there, the way it had haunted him last night, until finally he had decided that he must go back there this morning on the chance that she might still be there.

He told her everything. He was far too tired to weigh and measure words. He let the story pour from him like water from a sluice. As he talked he toyed with the rose paperweight, turning it over in his hand, looking down into the delicate bud at its center. Every now and then as he spoke, he would glance over at Gran. He had expected she would be angry, incredulous. But she seemed neither – she was only quiet, still, intent upon listening. The silence she left him allowed him to go on, filling it with fragments of this remarkable day.

He told her about going back to St. Bart's that morning and finding the girl still there, still lost. He told her about the trip to the restaurant, the library, the site of the old depot, the park, the trip back along the tracks. As he told the story, he stared into the rose weight and his fingers traced a pattern upon it. It started at the top, traveled down across the surface of the sphere to the base, then entered in imagination into the heart of the weight, circled there about the bud, then emerged again at the bottom to travel up the opposite side, and so end where it began. Circle within circle. Wheel within wheel.

The tale, as always, was altered in the telling. Things that had seemed unconnected before, now were neighbored. Remarks that had appeared unimportant, now assumed significance. He recollected things that had all but escaped his notice at the time, but now seemed central. It had all happened in such a rush and tumble. There had been no time to think. Now, in recollection, things assumed a pattern they had not appeared to possess.

As he drew near to the end of the story, he realized how utterly mad it must all have sounded. He set the weight back on the table, ran his hands through his hair, rubbed his stinging eyes. He was more tired than he could ever remember being before.

Gran sat silent for a few moments, while the story settled in.

"And where is this girl now?" she asked.

"Outside. In the shed."

"In the shed? Good heavens, boy, we must fetch the poor thing in at once."

She pushed herself up out of her chair. They walked together through the kitchen and out onto the porch, past the buggy hanging on its hook. The screen door slapped closed behind them.

With the setting of the sun, a chill had come into the air. Twilight had spun shadows through the yard. When he first opened the door of the shed he could see nothing, then the outline of an empty chair, a ball of silver lying on the seat of it.

"Ambriel," he called, thinking she might have hidden herself among the deeper shadows that clung about the corners of the shed. He walked in, plumbed all with his eyes, but the shed was empty. She was not there.

He plucked the silver ball from the seat of the empty chair. Gran's date squares.

"Ambriel," he called again, as though speaking her name might summon her forth.

"She's not here," he said, baffled, as he emerged from the shed. He searched every inch of the yard, squeezed back through the gap in the fence, called her name in both directions down the stretch of empty track. It was no good. She was gone.

Finally Gran took him by the arm and led him back into the house. He was chilled to the bone.

"She was there," he said hopelessly. "You have to believe me."

"I believe you," she said. "I believe you, Charles."

She sent him to his room to get a sweater. He pulled one on, then went and stood at the window and looked down at the shed. Soon all he could see was his own reflection, peering back at him from the glass.

Why had he not brought her in with him to begin with? Where could she have gone? He sat down on the edge of the bed, fingering the pendant around his neck, clinging to the small silver hand as if it were hers.

He lay back on the bed to rest his burning eyes – and was instantly asleep.

50

Midway through the night, something awakened him. He opened his eyes. The room was bathed in moonlight. He lay for a moment utterly disoriented, with no idea of what time it was, or why he was lying dressed in the dark. And then the memory of the day before came flooding back. He reached up and lightly touched his lip.

His shoes were lying paired by the bed. The quilt had been pulled up over him. Gran's work, no doubt. She must have come up to the room to check on him, found him asleep, and covered him up. As he lay piecing his thoughts together, he heard a light tapping on the glass. He looked over and saw Ambriel standing outside the window. He didn't stop to question how she could possibly be standing outside a second-story window. The impossibility of it did not appear to be a problem. All doubt and questioning were cast away by his sheer delight in seeing her again.

He went over and pulled open the sash and helped her in over the sill. She felt cool to the touch, like the coolness of the rose paperweight in his hand that night. She looked almost luminous as she stood there before him bathed in moonlight.

"I'm so glad to see you," he said. "I looked for you everywhere. I thought you'd gone."

"I could never leave you like that," she said. "Any more than you could leave me."

She went over and sat down on the edge of the bed. A cool breeze blew in through the open window. He closed it and went over to her.

"You must be cold," he said, and he drew the quilt up around her shoulders. She turned to him and smiled.

"I came to thank you," she said. "I remember now. I know the way home. I was sitting there in the shed, waiting. It was dark. But then suddenly the sun struck the little window; and the room lit up, and the walls seemed to fall away, and I remembered."

"I'm so glad," he said. But it was a lie. He wasn't glad at all. He was desperately sad at the thought of losing her.

"Is it far?" he asked.

"No, very near."

"Is it in Caledon?"

"Closer even than Caledon."

She took his hand in hers, and they spoke a long time together, though whether there were words, he could not say. It seemed rather that speech sprang from every pore of them.

Then suddenly she rose and walked toward the window, and the quilt fell from her shoulders to the floor.

"Don't leave."

"I will never leave you," she said, turning to him.

She held out her arms to him. He tried to stand, but it was as if he were frozen to the bed. He struggled with all his strength to rise. There was a sudden lurch, a dull thud –

He woke to find it morning and the first sun streaming into the room. Splayed on the floor by the bed lay the *Wonder Book*. The noise of its falling must have awakened him. The dream had been so achingly real. He looked about the room to assure himself she was not there.

He had no idea what time it was. The clock sat on top of the dresser. Because he had not wound it, it had stopped in the night. A quick wave of panic washed over him before he remembered it was Sunday and there were no papers to do.

He closed his eyes and tried to catch what fragments of the dream he could before they drifted out of reach. He could hear the sound of her voice still. He could sense a slight disturbance at the edges of the room in the wake of her presence, as when a stone is dropped in a still pool the waves ride out in widening circles and lap against the shore.

He tried to salvage scraps of the words she had spoken from the subtle echoes that still sounded through the room. He had the sense that some revelation had occurred, lost to him now in the light of day.

He forced himself to sit up before he fell asleep again. He ached in places he didn't even know he had. He threw off the quilt that covered him and bent to pick up the book from where it had fallen on the floor.

And then he saw it – a bit of broken glass sitting on the windowsill. Anyone else who saw it there would no doubt have thrown it out. But for him it was the confirmation of everything.

He went and picked it up and turned it in his hand. It was a triangular piece of emerald-colored glass. He ran the tip of his thumb around it as he had so often seen Ambriel do. And instantly the whole of that remarkable day rose before him. And the edges of it were the edges of that day, and the spur of the points was the spur of that day against all that had been sleeping in him for so long.

He closed his eyes and he could feel the walking, the endless walking; could feel the heat enfold him; could hear the rhythmic creak of the buggy wheel. And he knew with a certainty past all doubt that she had been in the room with him last night while he slept. And that what he imagined he had heard, he *had* heard; that what he imagined he had seen, he *had* seen.

He took the glass and held it to the light. What had been opaque in his palm was suddenly translucent. The glass was streaked. A bit of grit was embedded in it near one of the points of the triangle. Two small bubbles were suspended near the center of it.

They had gathered many bits of glass during the course of their walk. Each one was distinct and spoke somehow of the place where they had found it. Still, he was sure he would not be able to distinguish more than a handful of them. This one, however, he was able to place instantly. Looking at it now, feeling the heft of it in his hand – the way it nestled so perfectly in his palm, the odd uneven texture of it – he was sitting again in the restaurant with Ambriel, and she had just pulled the piece from one of her pockets as she was going through them looking for ID.

It seemed to him now, in light of all that had happened afterward, that this bit of glass was in a way her ID. She was somehow this and all those other bits she had gathered, dropped into her jangling pockets, pieced between the webbed roots of the tree.

But this piece he held in his hand was the first piece. It had come from St. Bart's, one of those many bits of glass from the broken window in which he had first found her covered. As he stood there with it now, he felt sure she had left it as a sign. Not simply as a sign of her having been there with him in the night, but a sign as well of where she had gone. It was as if she was telling him in the silent way she spoke that she had discovered that the way back home for her led back to the place where they had begun.

51

St. Bart stood in the shadows at the rear of the church with his skin draped over his arm, as if he had just come in from the cold and slipped off his coat. His eyes were open as they had been all through the night. All but a handful of petals had fallen from the jar of forsythia at his feet, and the water had begun to turn rank. He seemed neither to notice nor to care. He stood watching with unwavering eyes as the rising sun lit the windows along the east wall of the nave, and the figures slumbering in the glass stirred to life.

Once, in the early evening of his watch, the stillness had been broken by the sound of footsteps on the stairs, and the caretaker had come limping down the aisle. He had searched along the sill of the broken window, on the bench beneath it, on the ground round about it. He was a long time at it, looking for something. But when at last he quit the search, his footsteps fading into the depths of the church, he still had not found it.

Mr. Berkeley had worked all night on the window. He was long past tired. His thoughts came thick and strange. There was a voice in him, which had grown louder as the night wore on, that counseled despair and spoke alluringly of sleep. He had resisted the voice and, with the coming of dawn, it had withered and fallen away.

And now the labor was over. He carried the window carefully up the steep steps and along the aisle of the nave. Yet it was not simply the care with which one would handle some delicate object one feared might break, but rather the care with which one would carry a child asleep against one's breast.

The figure in the glass had been his sole companion for many hours. He had shattered her image unwittingly, and slowly he had pieced it together again. He had started with the piece on which her face had been painted. He had set that at the center, and about it the rest had slowly found form.

Even in those first hours, when the task had appeared impossible, he had gazed on that serene face, the strong line of the lips, the still depths of the eyes, and it had urged him on. It was a face painted from life. Quite unlike those vague, disembodied faces that peered from the other windows, she was concrete, individual, achingly alive.

As he carried the window down the aisle now, he found himself plumbing the shadows with his eyes. That strange sense of presence he had felt through the dark hours was with him still. He set the mended window down on the same bench where he had found it broken two days before. He stood on the bench and began removing the square of plywood that covered the window opening.

With the heel of his hand, he worked loose the shims with which he had secured the wood. Dawnlight streamed in as he lifted the wood away, momentarily blinding him. Then, as if in a vision, he saw a figure framed by the window opening, standing on the grass outside. He was so startled that he almost dropped the piece of plywood.

The figure looked familiar. Then he saw the guitar slung across her back and recognized her as the girl he had seen lingering about the church last Friday evening. From the way she was standing there like that, he had the strange feeling she had been waiting for him. Or was that simply the fatigue thinking?

As he turned and lowered the piece of plywood to the bench, he wondered if perhaps the girl had been sleeping on the grounds of the church. It would not be the first time someone had sheltered through the night against the walls of St. Bart's. Many were the cold winter mornings that he would find some poor soul curled up in one of the window wells, or camped in the space at the foot of the stairs outside that led to the basement. It had been warm yesterday, but there was a chill in the air now. Perhaps she was waiting for him to open the doors so that she could slip in and warm herself awhile.

But when he straightened again and glanced out the window, she was gone – gone without a trace. He could no longer be sure what he was seeing and what he was purely imagining. Had he simply conjured the girl up from the dregs of one too many cups of tea? Still, before he headed back down to the basement to fetch his tools and a small bucket of cement, he went and unlocked the doors, poking his head out briefly to scan the vacant stretch of lawn.

The church was still empty on his return. He used a hammer and chisel to clear away the ragged bits of concrete that clung to the grooves of the window opening. As he swept up the loose debris, he prayed that the window would fit back into the opening.

He leaned down to pick up the window and saw someone standing at the rear of the church by the statue of St. Bartholomew. His first thought was that it was the girl he had seen outside, but as the figure moved from the shadows he was shocked to find it was not her at all. Instead it was a boy, the boy who had been coming Friday afternoons. He remembered he had seen him last Friday after the window had broken. But what on earth was he doing here at this hour of the day? They exchanged glances as the boy moved along the aisle and settled into one of the pews near the rear of the church.

Mr. Berkeley went back to work. He raised the window up and lifted it into the light. Instantly it was transformed. This long labor of glass and lead, this patchwork of pieces re-collected in darkness, woke from its slumber with the kiss of light upon it, and was one. He was numbed by the beauty of it.

Carefully he slid the panel deep into the groove on one side of the window opening, then eased it into position and centered the whole so that both sides were held by the stonework. He twisted together the copper ties that secured the panel to the one above, cemented the window in place, then cleaned it carefully till it gleamed in the light.

There. It was done. He climbed down off the bench and gazed up at his work. The girl in the glass looked off toward the rear of the church. The glow of light through the window was like the flush of life in her cheeks. He swore that if he stood there long enough, those pale lips would part in speech and she would bless him.

There was that of him now in the work. A slight skew to the features, a slight slant to the pattern that had not been there before, that bit of glass gone missing from her gown that he had patched with a piece from his own store of glass. They somehow made her even more real, these mementos of the fall she now bore.

He picked up the piece of board that had covered the opening and carried it off to the basement. He would come back for the rest. No trace of his work must remain – only the window, appearing to the casual observer the same as it had always been.

EPILOGUE

What we call the beginning is often the end
And to make an end is to make a beginning.
The end is where we start from.

T. S. Eliot, *Four Quartets*

The scar began at the base of the nail of his baby finger and ran halfway round. When you stroked it with the thumb of your other hand, there was a strange numbness to it, and when you squeezed the skin, the flesh around it turned red and the line of the scar stood white against it, and you could count how many stitches there were.

When he was sitting thinking, he had a habit of rubbing the scar. He sat rubbing it now, and a memory rose whole and spontaneous in his mind like a genie streaming from a lamp – the memory of that Saturday morning Emily and he had tried to fix the clock.

As he sat there in the stillness of St. Bart's, he could hear again the creak of the stairs as he tiptoed quietly down to her room. He could feel the heft of the clock as they lifted it down from the cold room shelf. He could hear the frightful whir of wheels as the escapement slipped. He could feel the pain pulsing through the pillow sham Emily had wrapped around his finger; could see her sitting on the edge of the bed, telling him time and time again how sorry she was as the tears streamed down her face.

It seemed to him now that she was crying for far more than the accident with the clock. It seemed to him now she was telling him she was sorry for all the half-remembered injuries that had gone before – and all the things that came after.

Each life was seamed with stitches. Each one was broken and mended, broken and mended again. On some, the stitches showed more than on others, but no one remained unscathed.

Ambriel. At the slightest noise, he turned his head and hoped to see her standing there. Had he been wrong in reading the bit of glass on the sill as a sign? He watched in fascination as the caretaker set the window back in place. It had been the breaking of the window that had begun the whole adventure. It seemed right that he should be here to see it restored.

After he had finished resetting the window, the caretaker stood silently before it for a long while. Then he took up the piece of wood that had covered the opening and disappeared with it down the aisle and through the door at the front. Charles listened to his footsteps fade into the depths of the old church.

The clock marked each passing minute with a soft click dropped into the silence like a stone into a pool. The light woke the windows one by one.

"Ambriel," he caught himself saying aloud, for the sense of her presence was almost palpable. He closed his eyes and tried to summon the memory of her in the room with him last night, but it had faded entirely.

He found his eyes drawn repeatedly to the mended window. There was a figure in the glass, but he could not make it out from where he sat. At last he rose and made his way haltingly along the length of an empty pew until he stood in the side aisle under the window.

The bench where he had found Ambriel covered in broken glass two days before was streaked now with flecks of colored light cast from the window. He reached out and ran his hand through them, then glanced up at the figure in the glass.

It was the image of a girl, a portrait in glass. She was gazing off toward the rear of the church, as if she too were expecting someone. On her head she wore a circlet of gold. Her hair fell loose and long. Her gown was green, trimmed with ermine and bordered at the neck with gold brocade. In her hand she held a lute. About her neck she wore a pendant of gold. Behind her, framing the medallion in which she was set, there was a wheel wound in oak leaves. A pattern of lilies had been worked in the four corner pieces of the panel.

He watched the play of light through the glass, marveling at the intricacy of the design. He thought of Ambriel piecing her bits of glass between the roots of the tree. He looked at the figure: the eyes half lowered, gazing off into the distance; the set of the mouth, serious, yet with a whisper of a smile playing at the corners of the lips. He stood transfixed, oblivious to the passage of time, wrapped in reverie.

"Beautiful, isn't she?"

He nearly jumped out of his skin. It was the caretaker, come quietly up behind him while he was standing there. It was the first time he'd heard him speak. He had an English accent. It reminded him a little of Gran's.

"Sorry to startle you, lad."

"That's okay," said Charles. "I guess I was daydreaming. I didn't hear you coming."

The caretaker looked seriously in need of sleep. Dark circles were etched about his eyes. "I've been working all weekend on this window. Darn near drove me buggy, I don't mind telling you," he said, smiling. "But it worked out pretty well, I suppose."

"It's lovely," said Charles, looking back up at it.

"Not quite the way it was before, I'm afraid. Some slight twist to it now that wasn't there before. Do you see?"

"No," said Charles, "not really. Do you know who it's supposed to be?"

"Well, that's a bit of a mystery, lad, I must say. You see, most of the saints have a symbol they're shown with, so you know who they are. See a chap carrying keys, and you know it's St. Peter. See someone carrying his skin over his arm, and you know straight off it's St. Bart. It's like a picture language, you see?"

"Yes, I see."

"So with this girl," said the caretaker, looking up at the window, "the lute makes you think it might be St. Cecilia, the patron saint of musicians. But then there's that wheel in behind her there, which makes you think it could be St. Catherine. Very popular with the common folk, St. Catherine was. Patron saint of spinners, carters, millers – anyone who worked with wheels. Then again, perhaps she's not a saint at all. Could be an angel, but there would usually be wings. It could be the Virgin, but then the color of the gown is all wrong for that.

"So she's a bit of a mystery, you see. I'm not sure who she's supposed to be. And she's not about to tell us. She's just who she is, I suppose."

"Yes."

"There was a piece missing. You see there, in the gown?"

"Yes, I see."

"I tried to match it as well as I could. Of course, it's not quite like the old glass. There's nothing quite like the old glass."

Charles nodded in agreement.

"Are you a fancier of glass then, lad?"

"Yes, I suppose I am," said Charles.

"I can always tell. Just the way you were standing here as I came up the aisle. Let me introduce myself. The name's Berkeley. George, to my friends." And he held out his hand.

"I'm Charles Endicott."

"Pleased to meet you, Charles."

They shook hands and chatted while Mr. Berkeley gathered up his tools. Charles asked him if he'd happened to see a girl about the church that morning.

"As a matter of fact, there was a girl," said the caretaker, and he told Charles about the girl with the guitar he'd seen standing outside the window.

"I thought she might come in," he said. "In fact, when I first saw you there, I thought it was her. I imagine she's wandered off somewhere. She might come back. They often do. A friend of yours, is she?"

"Yes," said Charles. "A friend."

Mr. Berkeley glanced up at the clock. "Well, I'd best be getting on with things," he said. "I hope we'll chat again."

They said good-bye, and Charles watched him walk off down the aisle with the tool box and the bucket of cement. A couple of people had wandered into the church. One of them had parked himself in a rear pew, along with his plastic bags, and promptly fallen asleep. A woman was saying the Stations, working her way slowly along the aisle.

He stood silently in front of the window for a while, staring up into the face of the girl in the glass. He thought of the portrait of the young queen on the plate that had fallen from the wall at home, her delicate dovelike neck, the pattern of rays that ran through the mended pieces. He thought of Gran sitting in her chair in the pool of lamplight, leafing through the clippings in the coronation album; thought of the picture he had taken from the top of the ladder of the queen vanishing into the tunnel; thought of those Sunday afternoons with Father, parked by the siding, waiting for the Transcontinental to pass. He thought of Emily and her cryptic postcards, and those Saturday mornings when he had slipped downstairs and she had read to him from the *Wonder Book*. He thought of Ambriel and him, the creak and bump of the buggy behind them as they walked the streets of Caledon in the heat.

All of these many pieces were part of the portrait that was him. To him fell the gathering of them, light and dark;

the piecing of the intricate pattern, molding it, melding it, making a whole of it. Memory.

He glanced up at the window again. He looked into the girl's eyes, and for a moment glimpsed the eyes behind those eyes, and thought of Ambriel.

"I'm glad you found your way home," he whispered to himself in the silence. Then he turned and made his way down the aisle, past the statue of St. Bart, and out the door into day.

As he blinked in the sudden light, he thought of walking out this same door yesterday with Ambriel in tow. He remembered the way she had hesitated in the doorway, as if she was afraid to go on. He seemed to feel her there beside him now as he made his way down the stairs.

Halfway down, he spotted a piece of glass lying on a step. A bit of blue glass, from the base of a bottle, it seemed. You didn't see much blue about. He stooped to pick it up.

The End